A Will to Survive

The Hardys turned off Red Ribbon Trail onto an unmarked side path.

Joe understood why this path was kept off-limits to visitors. It led right along the edge of the bluff. Leaning over, he could see the narrow beach and surf—damp rocks sixty feet below.

"There's the summerhouse," Frank said. The rustic building perched at the very tip of a protruding section of the bluff, with views on three sides. "You realize this is a trap."

"Sure," Joe replied. "Why don't we leave the path before we get there and come on it from the other direction? Maybe we can get a look at whoever's waiting to ambush us."

"Lead on," Frank said, with an ironic bow.

Joe edged past him. He had taken only a few steps when he felt the ground collapse under him. Caught off balance, he started to tumble down the steep bluff to the deadly rocks far below.

The Hardy Boys Mystery Stories

Available from MINSTREL Books

THE HARDY BOYS®

156

A WILL TO SURVIVE

FRANKLIN W. DIXON

A MINSTREL® BOOK

Published by POCKET BOOKS

New York   London   Toronto   Sydney   Tokyo   Singapore

A MINSTREL PAPERBACK *Original*

 A Minstrel Book published by
POCKET BOOKS, a division of Simon & Schuster Inc.
1230 Avenue of the Americas, New York, NY 10020

Copyright © 1999 by Simon & Schuster Inc.

Front cover illustration by Broeck Steadman

All rights reserved, including the right to reproduce this book or portions thereof in any form whatsoever. For information address Pocket Books, 1230 Avenue of the Americas, New York, NY 10020

ISBN: 0-671-03464-2

First Minstrel Books printing May 1999

10   9   8   7   6   5   4   3   2   1

THE HARDY BOYS MYSTERY STORIES is a trademark of Simon & Schuster Inc.

THE HARDY BOYS, A MINSTREL BOOK and colophon are registered trademarks of Simon & Schuster Inc.

Printed in the U.S.A.

Contents

A WILL TO SURVIVE

1 Nature Preserved

"All of this land along here is part of Shorewood Nature Center," Callie Shaw said from the front seat of Frank Hardy's van. "There's the entrance, up ahead on the right."

It was early on a Monday morning in June. Frank was at the wheel of the van. He glanced over at the high stone wall that ran along the road. It seemed to stretch on forever. On the other side of the wall, thick trees loomed faintly in the patchy morning mist. "The place must be enormous," he remarked.

"It's more than half the size of New York's Central Park," Callie replied. "It's big enough to get lost in, anyway."

"Big enough to hide somebody who's up to no good," Joe Hardy observed from the backseat. "I'm glad you came by yesterday to tell us you've been having these problems."

"So am I," Callie replied. "The summer intern program kicked off just about three weeks ago, at the beginning of the month. Those spooky noises began practically the first night all the interns got to the center."

"Maybe one of you brought the spooky noises with him . . . or her," Joe said.

Callie nodded. "I thought of that. But until we arrived, no one was staying in the main part of the house. It was totally empty after dark. What if there were suspicious noises? Nobody was there to notice them."

"Old houses always have weird squeaks and creaks," Frank pointed out. He slowed the van and put on his turn signal. Tall stone pillars flanked the narrow entrance. As he steered the van between them, he caught a glimpse of a weathered coat of arms carved into the one on the right.

"Sure," Callie said. She reached over to touch his arm. "I wouldn't have asked you and Joe to help if that were all we're dealing with. But it's not just noises. The furniture moves around. Last night a display case of rare lizards was knocked over."

"Leaping lizards!" Joe exclaimed.

Callie chuckled. "I thought of that, too," she said. "But I'm afraid it's no joke. A lot of tension has built up. We're snapping at one another. Some of the visitors are starting to notice. If we don't . . ."

"Wha—" Frank gripped the wheel tighter and

slammed on the brake. The van juddered to a stop. Twenty feet ahead, in the mist, a huge dark form ambled across the road and vanished into the woods.

"What in the world?" Joe demanded. "I could swear that was a moose!"

Callie giggled. "It *was* a moose."

Frank cautiously put the van in motion. "Oh sure, a moose. I knew that," he said. "But what's a moose doing down here? I usually think of them as belonging somewhere up north."

"That is where most of them live now," Callie explained. "But back before this area was settled, this was at the southern end of their range. Now Shorewood is bringing them back. We've got a whole family of mooses . . . I mean, moose. You have to be careful driving around the grounds. They might not get out of the way of your car."

"Why should they?" Joe cracked. "They're probably bigger than your car. *You* should get out of *their* way."

"Hey, Joe, you're starting to think like a Shorewood intern," Callie said with a smile. "We should learn from nature and adapt to it, not expect nature to adapt to us."

The road wound through the woods and crossed a meadow where a flock of sheep grazed. Joe leaned out the window and went *"Baa-a-a!"* A few sheep looked up, then went back to chomping grass.

"Don't take this adapting business *too* seriously,

Joe," Callie warned him. Her voice went into a singsong. "Rule Two: Don't disturb the animals."

"What's Rule One?" asked Frank.

Callie grinned. "No bad jokes."

"I have the feeling that's *Callie's* Rule One," Joe said with a sly smile.

As they rounded a curve, Frank spotted the main house through the trees. He gave a soft whistle. A moment later Joe echoed him.

Built of stone the color of dark honey, Shorewood was three stories high and wide enough to fill the full length of a football field. A dozen or more ornate brick chimneys pierced the weathered green copper roof.

The long rows of tall windows overlooked the precise lines of a formal garden. In the center of the garden, four stone statues of sea monsters spouted streams of water into a reflecting pool. Beyond the house, through a break in the trees, the waters of the bay gleamed in the distance.

"What a dump," Joe said, sounding impressed in spite of his words.

"It's actually pretty modest, compared to some of the really big old estates around here," Callie replied. "Shorewood's known more for the grounds than for the house. Still, it's big enough to make a really nice museum and still have plenty of room to house the internship program. But can you imagine living in a place this size all by yourself, the way old Mr. Parent did? Brr-r-r!"

4

Frank drove to the back of the building and followed signs to the staff parking lot. This was a paved brick area surrounded on three sides by a stable, an eight-car garage with a clock tower, and what must have been a guest cottage or servants' quarters. Frank parked next to a green pickup truck with the Shorewood crest on the door.

The three friends walked to the house and entered through a glassed-in porch. The peeling wicker chairs and couches looked as if no one had sat on them for years. French doors opened onto a wide entrance hall dominated by a curving staircase. On the wall to the right hung an enormous painting of assorted wild animals. Frank identified some turtles, an antlered deer, and a variety of birds.

Callie noticed Frank's interest. "That's by Walter Parent, the guy who set up Shorewood," she said. "Wildlife painting was one of his hobbies."

"I figured it had to be a hobby," Joe said. "If the rest of his paintings were as bad as that one, no way he could have made enough money to build a place like this."

"Watch out, Joe," Callie said. "What if his ghost hears you? He might arrange for something to fall on your head—or even worse, on mine!"

The Hardys followed Callie down an echoey hallway to a tall, gleaming mahogany door. She tapped once and pushed the door open.

"Ah, Callie, you're back," a low voice said. Frank

thought he heard a slight Eastern European accent. "Good. And these are your friends who are willing to help us out. Come in, come in."

Callie led the way inside. "Tanya, meet Frank and Joe Hardy," she said. "Guys, this is Tanya Sovskaya, Shorewood's director."

Tanya seemed younger than Frank had expected the center's director to be. He put her age at about thirty-five. She had a roundish face framed by light brown hair that stopped just above her shoulders.

"Please sit down," Tanya said, waving to three chairs that faced her desk. "I'm glad to meet you. I am very impressed by what Callie has told me about your exploits as detectives. And I just finished hearing your praises from a member of our board who is acquainted with your father."

Fenton Hardy, a famous private detective, had enlisted the help of his two sons on many tough cases. It had been natural for Frank and Joe to start investigating crimes and solving mysteries on their own. Though they were still teenagers, they had growing reputations as skilled detectives.

"Dad's taught us a lot," Joe said.

"You're being modest. From what I've heard, you've learned it very well," Tanya replied. "I must say I hesitated. Your youth, after all . . ."

She picked up a pen and rolled it between her fingers for a few moments. Then she tapped it decisively on the polished surface of the desk. "However, that may work to our advantage," she continued. "Are you willing to pretend to join the internship program? You will fit right in. No one will suspect you're investigating the strange goings-on. You will gain an insider's view that no adult investigator could hope for. It may not be easy to play such a role, of course. . . ."

"We've done this type of thing before," Frank assured her. "And we'll have Callie to help us."

"That's right," Callie interjected. "I mean, everyone knows that I live close enough to Shore-wood to go home on Sundays. It's perfectly logical that I've gotten them interested in the program, and so here they are being interviewed."

"Callie's told us a little about what's been going on," Joe added. "It doesn't sound very dangerous. Why do you want us to look into it? Why not handle it yourselves?"

Tanya sighed. "If these pranks were the only problem, perhaps I would. In itself, such mischief is a minor irritation. It is no worse than, say, discovering a patch of poison ivy along one of the footpaths. But we face a complex situation. Do you know the history of Shorewood Nature Center?"

"Uh-uh," Frank and Joe said together.

"We've been in existence for less than two years," Tanya explained. "All this was the idea of a wealthy nature lover named Walter Parent, who set up the center in his will."

"The guy who did that big animal painting in the hall?" Frank asked.

"That's right. His will stipulates that the painting stay on display. He was obviously very proud of it."

"I can't imagine why," Callie commented. "It's not very good."

Tanya gave a small smile. "Parent had a number of interests," she said. "Nature painting was one of them. Another was puzzles. We have several shelves of puzzle books in the library, along with cabinets full of jigsaw and other puzzles."

"He had another hobby, too," Callie said. "Changing his will. Every time he got angry at someone or read something in the paper he didn't like, he'd write a new will. Good thing he never lost interest in nature study—he might have left everything to a foundation to study perpetual motion."

"He sounds a little, well, eccentric," Frank said.

"It's not my place to judge Walter Parent," Tanya said. "His final will did great good by establishing this center. However, his fortune was not nearly as large as he may have believed. The house and land are immensely valuable, of course, but aside from that, the center's resources are stretched very thin."

"You mean, there wasn't as much money in his estate as you expected?" Frank asked.

Tanya took a deep breath. "That's correct," she said. "In fact, our endowment is several million dollars less than we had been led to believe it would be."

Joe's eyebrows shot up in astonishment. "Several million? Where did it go?" he asked. "You don't lose that kind of money from having it roll under the dresser."

"Who knows?" Tanya said with a shrug. "Perhaps he made poor investments. Perhaps there never was as much as he thought. In any case, we depend much more on support from the community than would have been the case. We are a new institution, still building a positive image and reputation. Anything that threatens our good name could be disastrous."

"That makes sense," Frank said. "But how   "

Tanya's telephone buzzed. Frank broke off what he was saying while she answered it.

"Yes, Roger," she said. "Yes, I got your letter. Just a moment." She covered the mouthpiece and said, "This may take a few minutes. Callie, why don't you show Joe and Frank around the grounds?"

Frank, Joe, and Callie got to their feet and headed for the door. As they left the room, Frank overheard Tanya say, "Now, Roger, what is this nonsense about selling our water frontage? You know how crucial the shoreline is to the mission of the center."

Frank made a mental note to find out more about the center's financial difficulties.

Callie led Frank and Joe out a side door. By now the mist had lifted, and the day had become sunny. "Let's take a look at the Heirloom Garden," Callie suggested. "That's where we're working to revive old-time varieties of flowers and vegetables. These are kinds our great-grandparents grew that almost died out when people turned to modern hybrids."

They followed a stone walk that curved across the lawn. On the other side of a stand of fir trees was an enclosure surrounded by a dusky redbrick wall. The walk led to an arched gateway in the wall.

As they started through, Frank heard a deep voice say, "Don't be an idiot, Jack. I never touched your stupid cucumbers."

The Hardys hurried forward. Two teenagers were confronting each other amid the rows of vegetables. One was short and stocky, with dark hair. The other, who Frank figured was Jack, was taller and thinner, with a blond crew cut. He was gripping a spade with enough force to turn his knuckles white.

"Touch them? You destroyed them!" Jack accused, sticking out his chin. "It's all part of your plan, isn't it, Sal? You're part of some kind of plot to destroy the center!"

"You're out of your mind, Jack," Sal replied. "Get a grip, man." He turned to walk away.

Jack's face reddened. The veins in his neck bulged. He stood still as Sal took several steps. Then, suddenly, before Joe, Frank, or Callie could do anything to stop him he lifted the sharp spade over his head and started to swing it at the back of Sal's head.

2 Trampled Cukes

"Sal!" Callie screamed. "Look out!"

The sun glinted off the steel blade as the spade arced down at the unsuspecting Sal.

Joe sprinted across the garden, leaping over the rows of plants like a hurdler. When he was still a couple of strides away, he realized that he was not going to reach the attacker in time. Stretching out his arms, he launched himself into a desperate leap.

Joe's left hand slammed into the wooden shaft of the spade. Ignoring the stinging pain in his palm, he kept a tight grip on the tool. As he tucked into a roll, he wrenched the spade out of the surprised Jack's hands and flung it as far as he could across the garden.

As he hit the ground, Joe got his feet under him and bounced up, twisting to face Jack. But Frank and Callie were already on the scene. Frank was holding Jack by the shoulders, and Callie was pulling the now-furious Sal away.

"Cool down, pal," Frank told Jack. "Take a deep breath."

"You toad!" Sal shouted, shaking his fist at Jack. He tried to pull away from Callie's grip. "Are you totally nuts? You could have killed me with that thing!"

Joe placed himself between Sal and Jack. He wanted to be ready in case one of them decided to get physical again.

Jack took a deep breath, then shook his head from side to side. "Look, I'm sorry, Sal," he muttered. "I don't know what came over me. I didn't even know I had that spade in my hands."

"You shouldn't be let out alone," Sal said. He sounded slightly calmer. "If it hadn't been for these guys . . ."

"What got you two started anyway?" asked Callie. "I thought you were friends."

"We had a bet going about whose vegetables would grow better," Jack explained. "Sal kept teasing me about how he would win. So when I discovered somebody had tromped on my cukes, I got really mad."

"I never touched your cucumbers," Sal insisted, his voice rising. "Why would I do that?"

"Why would anybody?" Jack retorted. "But look for yourself—*somebody* did."

Joe looked. Jack was right. The young vines had been trampled into the ground. The damage looked too thorough to have been done by accident.

"What about a moose?" Callie suggested. "They weigh about a ton. Maybe one of them got into the garden."

Frank got down on one knee next to the cucumbers. He studied the marks in the dirt. "A moose wearing cross-training shoes?" he said. "I don't think so."

Sal pointed to his light brown work boots and said, "These clod-stompers didn't make those prints, that's for sure. Well, Jack?"

"I guess I was way out of line," Jack mumbled. "I'm sorry, Sal. But if I find out who murdered my cukes, I'll ram a full-grown zucchini down his throat—and that's just for starters!" Not looking at Joe or Frank, he walked over to retrieve his spade. Then he went to a far corner and started digging.

"Hey, I owe you guys," Sal said with a quick smile. "Are these the friends of yours who live nearby, Callie?"

"That's right." Callie introduced Joe and Frank, then went on. "I talked them into signing on as interns. In fact, they're supposed to be in talking to Tanya right now. She must be wondering what I did with them. We'd better get back."

"Okay," Sal said. "Welcome aboard, Joe, Frank. I'll catch you later." He went back to weeding his plants.

Tanya was just hanging up the phone when the

three reentered her office. Joe glimpsed an expression of concern mixed with anger on her face. She seemed to will it away and asked, "Did you enjoy your walk?"

"It was very interesting," Frank told her. "This is quite a place." He didn't mention the near-battle between Jack and Sal, and gave Joe a look that seemed to tell him not to let anything slip about it either.

"This could be a *great* place," Tanya replied, slapping her palm on her desktop. "It will be, if we're allowed to survive. I cannot fathom why anyone would want to wreck what we're building here. What could the motive be?"

"Could it be resentment?" Joe suggested. "A new operation this big, there must have been some opposition."

"Well . . . at first, perhaps," Tanya admitted. "Some neighbors were worried about increased traffic. Others didn't like the fact that such a huge estate would no longer pay the town any taxes. But we brought them around. We built a new entrance for groups, which cut down on local traffic. And our studies showed that the growth from our presence here would more than make up for the lost taxes."

Frank scratched his cheek. "Callie said before that Walter Parent liked to change his will. There must be people who expected a legacy they didn't get. Maybe they resent the center for getting the money they were counting on."

Tanya gave a wry smile. "Anyone who dealt with Walter knew not to count on anything," she said. "I

14

sometimes think that watching us jump through hoops for him was the only entertainment he got. Walter and I must have met dozens of times to draw up detailed plans for Shorewood Nature Center. Even so, I was not really convinced it would happen until after his death, when the will was read."

"Did he have any family?" Joe asked.

"He had a distant cousin," Tanya replied. "They were not on speaking terms and hadn't been for years. It was some old quarrel, I imagine. In any case, how would destroying the work of Shorewood benefit a distant relative? It makes no sense."

"We're just trying to make sure we cover all the bases," Frank told her.

"I understand, and I appreciate that," Tanya said. "This means that you're going to help us. I can't thank you enough. When can you start?"

Joe grinned. "Thanks to Callie, we came prepared. We've got our bags out in the van."

"We let our parents know we would be away for a few days," Frank added.

"Excellent," Tanya said. She pushed her chair back and stood up. "Callie, will you take Frank and Joe to meet Bruce? I'll let him know to expect you."

As they started for the door, Tanya said, "Wait a moment." She rummaged through a file cabinet and took out some papers. Putting them in a manila envelope, she continued, "These are some of the letters Parent wrote me when we were planning the center. They may give you a clearer idea of his plans—as well as his quirky personality."

As they walked down the hall, Callie said, "I'm going to hand you over to Bruce Rotan now. He's the assistant director. Anything you want to know about the history of this place, Bruce is the guy to ask. He was Parent's private secretary for years."

Joe thought that a former private secretary to an eccentric millionaire would be tall, thin, and middle-aged, with a habit of saying "Um" and "Er." Bruce Rotan did not look as if he had hit thirty yet. He had thick black hair and an aggressive jaw. His tight yellow polo shirt showed off muscles that obviously owed a lot to work in the gym.

"Welcome!" he said, offering his hand to Frank. Joe noticed that he squeezed harder than he needed to. When he turned to Joe, Joe was ready for him. He squeezed back every bit as heartily. Bruce's smile developed a slight edge.

"Let's get you settled in," Bruce continued, flipping through some papers. "Joe, you'll be rooming with a fellow named Sal Politano. Frank, I'm putting you in a triple, with Jack Mainwaring and Rahsaan Jefferson. I'll show you the rooms in a few minutes, and you can meet your roommates at dinner."

"We've already met Sal and Jack," Frank said.

"That's right," Joe said, keeping his voice neutral.

"Oh? Good, that's a start," Bruce said. "Here's a sheet with meal hours, house rules, important phone numbers, and so on. The way we work it, all

16

the interns attend a seminar in the morning before the center opens to the public. We take up a different aspect of the center's work each day. Don't even *think* about skipping one!"

"No, of course not," Frank murmured.

"Our interns get a lot of varied and valuable experience," Bruce continued. "You'll guide visitors around the house and grounds, go out into the community to make presentations, and help with ongoing ecological research. You might spend one morning learning forestry management and the afternoon shearing sheep."

"I don't know how to shear a sheep," Joe remarked uneasily.

Bruce grinned. "You'll learn fast. Our system is, 'Each one teach one.' Someone who doesn't have a particular craft or skill will be paired with someone who does. Your first few days, you'll simply observe. Then you'll get to try what you've learned. You'll be supervised, of course. If you do okay, after that you're on your own."

He glanced at his watch. "I'd better get you moved in. Go get your things and meet me in the entrance hall. You'll just have time to unpack before dinner. When you hear the bell, head for the dining room. It's in the basement."

The dorm rooms, on the third floor, were furnished simply but comfortably with a single bed and small dresser for each occupant. "No bunk beds," Joe observed. "That's a relief. I don't know which is worse, the top bunk or the bottom bunk."

"The bottom," Frank said with a chuckle. "Take my word for it—anyone who's had a little brother tossing and turning on the top bunk when they were kids will tell you that."

Frank neatly ducked Joe's punch, then said, "Let's put away our stuff and do some more exploring before dinner."

A few minutes later, they started down the stairs. At the second-floor landing, they met a tall, thin guy in baggy jeans and a sweatshirt with the logo of a famous designer on the front.

"Hey!" the guy said. "You must be the newbies I heard about. I'm Rahsaan. Which of you gets the honor of sharing a room with me and Jack?"

"That would be me," Frank said. "Frank Hardy. And this is my brother, Joe."

"Frank and Joe Hardy . . ." Rahsaan wrinkled his forehead. "Do I know you dudes from somewhere? You don't look familiar, but . . . Oh well, it'll come to me."

Joe exchanged a glance with Frank. Did Rahsaan know them? Had he heard stories about their previous detective work? If so, would he blow their cover? They would have to keep a close watch on the situation.

"Where're you headed?" Rahsaan asked them. As if in answer, a bell clanged two floors below.

"Dinnertime," Rahsaan said. "Hey, you want to see something really cool first?" He walked a few steps down the corridor and pressed against one of

18

the wood panels. A section of paneling swung inward.

"Wow!" Joe exclaimed. "Look at that—a hidden staircase! Incredible! I love stuff like that."

"Me, too," Rahsaan said. "Back when these places were built, the servants weren't supposed to be seen *or* heard. They had their own network of hallways and stairways. That way, they could get wherever they had to go without disturbing the high muckety-mucks. Wouldn't you love to play hide-and-seek around here? The game could go on for weeks!"

Joe and Frank followed Rahsaan down the narrow, dimly lit stairs. At the bottom was a bright corridor with bare plaster walls. From the right they could hear the clatter of pots and pans, and from the left, the rattle of dishes and the hum of voices. They turned left.

The staff dining room was a big, high-ceilinged space dominated by a long wooden table. Glass-front cabinets stacked with china and glassware reached nearly to the ceiling. Half a dozen people were standing around. Joe recognized Sal and Jack.

Callie hurried over. "Oh, great, you found your way," she said. "I'm on carrying duty tonight—we all take turns—but come meet my roommate, Wendy Chen."

Wendy had a welcoming smile and long black hair that kept drifting in front of her face. She was wearing jeans and a T-shirt from the most recent tour of a hot new band. "Come on and sit down," she said, after greeting Joe and Frank. "Breakfast and lunch are buffets, but dinner's served family style. It's a great way to get to know everyone."

Joe noticed that Tanya, Bruce, and two other adults sat at the far end of the table, while the teen interns clustered at the near end. He took the place next to Wendy. Sal was across from him.

"I hear we're roommates," Joe said in a friendly tone.

"Um," Sal replied. "Yeah." He seemed preoccupied.

Joe spent the rest of the meal talking to Frank, Wendy, and Rahsaan. Afterward, everyone helped clear the table, then went to another room furnished with chairs, sofas, game tables, and a big TV.

Joe tried again to make some contact with Sal. He had no more luck than he did at dinner. He decided to use his energy getting to know some of the others instead. Before very long it was time to turn in.

Joe tossed and turned for what seemed like hours. Finally he sat up in bed. The glowing dial on his watch said 3:14. Maybe a glass of water would help him sleep. He slipped into his clothes and tiptoed toward the door. As he passed Sal's bed, he noticed it was empty. So he wasn't the only one who was having trouble sleeping!

Joe stepped into the hallway. Suddenly he stopped and stood motionless, listening intently.

From somewhere in the distance came a scraping noise. It sounded like something heavy being dragged across the floor. It was coming from downstairs.

Joe hesitated. Should he wake Frank? No, there was too much risk of waking Frank's roommates as well. Joe ran quietly down the stairs to the entrance hall. The heavy silence was unbroken, and the dim security lights did not reveal anything suspicious.

Joe stepped inside the first of the exhibit rooms. As he did, he sensed a presence near him. He started to turn. At that moment, a muscular arm wrapped itself around his neck, then tightened.

Joe struggled for breath. A red film started to descend over his vision.

3 The Secret in the Wall

Joe reached up and clamped both hands on the arm that was strangling him. He tensed, preparing to drop to one knee and throw his attacker over his shoulder. Then he recalled that the room in front of him was filled with glass display cases. Could he take the risk of destroying dozens of precious museum specimens?

On the other hand, could he take the risk of allowing somebody to throttle him? If he didn't do something at once, he might not have the strength to save himself!

To buy time, Joe lifted his right foot and stamped down where he thought his assailant's foot must be. He aim was perfect, but he had forgotten he was barefoot. The other guy wasn't. From the pain in his heel, Joe guessed the other guy was wearing steel-toed work boots.

Joe let himself go limp and slump forward, as if starting to pass out. His attacker leaned forward with him. Instantly Joe used his powerful neck muscles to thrust his head backward. The back of his head struck something with a satisfying crunch, followed by a gasp of pain.

The arm around Joe's neck loosened just enough for him to force his fingers under it. He drew in one quick, welcome breath. Then, before his attacker could recover, he threw all his weight and all the strength of his linebacker's legs into a backward push. After two steps, he felt the other guy slam into a wall. The arm fell away from Joe's throat.

Joe hurled himself away. Spinning on one foot to face his opponent, he dropped into a defensive posture. He raised both hands, ready to strike out with devastating force.

The lights clicked on, blinding him for a moment. A voice he recognized as Tanya's shouted, "Carl! Joe! What's going on here? Stop it at once!"

Tanya was standing in the entrance hall, with a small group behind her.

The man who had tried to choke Joe was a balding six-footer with powerful shoulders and a thick neck. The sleeves on his frayed khaki shirt were rolled up above the elbow, showing a sharp border between his deeply tanned forearms and pale upper arms.

"I caught this fellow prowling around, Ms. Sovskaya," he said. "He wouldn't come quietly." He reached up to rub a bright red patch on his left cheek.

"I woke up and heard a noise down here," Joe explained. "I came to see what it was. This guy jumped me from behind and tried to strangle me."

Frank pushed through the crowd and came over to Joe's side. "Are you okay?" he asked in an undertone.

Joe massaged the side of his throat. "I'll probably be a little sore tomorrow," he said cheerfully. "But not as sore as that guy."

"I see," Tanya said, raising her voice. "This is all an unfortunate misunderstanding. Carl, that is Joe Hardy, a new intern. Joe, Carl is our caretaker. He is in charge of the upkeep of the house and grounds. As you can see, he takes his job very seriously."

"Yeah, I can see that," Joe said. To himself, he wondered if Carl's duties always involved lurking around the house at three in the morning.

"All right, everyone," Tanya continued. "The excitement is over. Please return to your rooms. We have much to do tomorrow."

Joe shot Tanya a quick, imploring glance. She noticed and understood.

"Joe, Frank," she said, as the others started drifting upstairs. "Will you stay for a moment? I need to speak to you. Carl, you may go. I'll see you in the morning."

After an unfriendly look at Joe, Carl left the Hardys alone with Tanya.

In a low voice, Joe said, "I *did* hear something down here. It sounded like furniture being shifted around. I'd like to know what it was."

"So would I," Tanya agreed. "Will you and Frank see what you can discover? I'll wait here, in case anyone else returns and wonders what you're doing."

"We weren't in this room during our look around earlier," Frank told her. "Can you tell us if anything catches your attention? Don't work at noticing, just let your eyes and your mind roam."

"Very well." Tanya walked to the center of the room and slowly turned, letting her gaze move from one corner of the room to another. Finally she said, "The elk. I don't think its head always pointed exactly in that direction."

Frank followed the direction of her eyes. The stuffed elk was hard to miss. It was mounted on a solid platform painted to look like grass. Its head was raised, as if listening for danger. Its antlers reached almost to the ceiling.

Frank and Joe crossed the room. Joe peered down at the floor. "Look, Frank," he said excitedly. "Those scratches are fresh!"

A series of parallel scratches showed yellowish on the dark polished floorboards. Frank estimated that the scratches were a bit under a foot long. It looked as if someone had shoved the front of the elk's stand over, pivoting it on the rear part.

"Give me a hand," Frank said. He and Joe knelt down to push the elk's platform. There was a teeth-gritting screech as the metal scraped across the wooden floor. They stopped at once.

"That's the sound I heard earlier," Joe said. "So somebody moved the elk . . . but why?"

The two detectives studied the placement of the elk. "The only reason I can come up with," Frank said slowly, "is to get to the wall behind the exhibit. I wonder . . ."

With his knuckles, Frank tapped on the carved wooden paneling. He started as high as he could reach and slowly moved down toward the floor. When he got to chest level, the sound changed.

"It must be hollow behind this spot!" Frank exclaimed. He felt the borders of the panel with his fingertips. Was that a crack? He tried to get his thumbnail into it. There was a faint click. The panel swung outward. Behind it, built into the wall, was a cabinet with two shelves. Eagerly Frank leaned forward to peer inside. All he saw was a furry layer of dust and a few dead flies.

"We're too late," Joe said bitterly. "If only I'd gotten here a couple of minutes sooner!"

Frank took a closer look at the shelves. "Give yourself a break," he said. "Getting here sooner wouldn't have helped. Nothing's disturbed this dust for a long time."

Glancing over his shoulder at Tanya, Frank asked, "Did you know this compartment was here?"

Tanya shook her head. "This one, no. But it

26

doesn't surprise me. The house has many secret doors and stairways. There is a compartment like that in my office I use to store checks."

"Does everybody know about these secret cabinets?" asked Joe. "I mean, that they exist."

"It is part of the lore of the place, like the servants' stairs," Tanya told him. "It's not a secret, exactly, but an unusual and interesting feature."

"Hmm." Frank scratched his chin. "Is there a blueprint of the building that would show us where they are?"

"We have the plans that were drawn up when we converted the mansion," Tanya replied. "But they indicate only those compartments that our architects knew about. This one, for example, is not shown."

"Still, we should look at the plan in the morning," Frank said. He added, "I don't know that we can do much more now. And we don't want the others to wonder what we're doing down here."

As Frank and Joe started up the stairs, Joe stopped his brother. "I didn't want to tell you this with the others around. When I got out of bed, I was careful not to wake Sal. But the moonlight coming in the window was shining on his bed . . . and he wasn't there."

"You think he—" Frank began.

Joe finished the thought. "Was downstairs hunting for the secret compartment? Could be. We'd better keep a careful eye on him."

"And who better to do that than his roommate?"

Frank said, slapping Joe on the shoulder. "Starting right now!"

After breakfast only a few hours later, Frank and Joe joined the other interns in the seminar room. The speaker was a marine biologist from the state university. She spoke about the many life-forms that make their home on the strip of beach between the high-tide and low-tide marks. Colorful slides and videos illustrated the talk. By the end Frank knew he would never look at a beach the same way again. It was so much more than just a place to lie on the sand and bag some rays!

Bruce caught up to Frank and Joe as they left the seminar. "Wendy is leading a junior-high-school group around the indoor exhibits this morning," he said. "I'd like you two to join the group. You'll get a good introduction to the center and pick up some pointers on handling this kind of assignment at the same time."

"Sounds good," Joe said.

They found Wendy in the entrance hall, talking to a guy of about seventeen with shaggy brown hair and a round face. For some reason he made Frank think of a cocker spaniel. Maybe it was his earnest brown eyes.

Frank explained to Wendy about the assignment Bruce had given them. "I hope that's not a drag for you," he said apologetically.

"No problem," Wendy said. "Hey, this is a friend of mine, Dylan Silver. He's coming on the tour, too.

Frank and Joe are new interns. This is their first day."

"You're not in the program?" Joe asked Dylan.

"No," Dylan replied. "It seems really interesting, though." From the look on his face when he glanced at Wendy, Frank thought he could guess what Dylan's main interest was.

A group of about fifteen junior-high-school students came in. It was time for the tour. Wendy guided the group through the rooms on the first floor, explaining the maps of bird migration routes and pointing out rare specimens on display. Frank only half-listened. He was busy examining the walls for clues to the location of hidden compartments. He spotted several possibilities that he planned to come back and check out later.

The students were trying an ecology computer game when Tanya came into the room. She beckoned Frank and Joe over. "Can I see you in my office?" she said.

They followed her out. Frank was aware of curious glances from Wendy and Dylan. They probably thought the Hardys were in some sort of trouble.

Tanya closed her office door, then went to her desk. "Listen to this," she said, pressing the Play button on her answering machine.

A woman's voice said, "Hello, this is Kate Mulhare, with Channel Eight news. I understand that Shorewood Nature Center is having problems with a poltergeist—bumps in the night, display animals moving around, and other strange incidents. I'd like to set a time to interview you and see when we can bring a crew out to shoot some footage."

"This is exactly the sort of publicity that could do us in!" Tanya exclaimed. "Who would want to tip off the press? It must be someone who knows all about this harassment campaign."

"Who knows better than the person who's behind it?" Joe asked.

"I see that," Tanya replied. "But where does it take us? Can we find out who made the call?"

"We've dealt with a few local reporters in the past," Frank said. "We could call one or two and ask if they've been in touch with the tipster. But if we do, we'll probably just convince them that there's a good story in it."

"I see," Tanya said. She sighed. "No, we do not want that. I suppose I must talk to this woman from Channel Eight. Perhaps I can make what is happening seem very ordinary."

"The main thing," Joe suggested, "is not to sound like you're hiding anything. Reporters start to drool when they think someone's trying to hide something from them."

As he and Joe left Tanya's office, Frank checked his watch. "It's too late to rejoin the tour, but we still have some free time before lunch," he said. "How about we look over those letters from Parent that Tanya gave us?"

"Where did you put them?" Joe asked. "Not where anybody might spot them, I hope."

"In your dreams," Frank retorted. "The envelope's tucked into a magazine at the bottom of my bag. And I rested a hair across the zipper, so I'll know if anyone's been prying."

Frank went upstairs and returned with the envelope. He and Joe walked outside to a bench in the shade of a spreading oak tree with a view of the house and lawn. They divided up the letters and started reading.

After a few minutes, Joe gave a snort.

"What?" Frank asked, looking up.

"This guy had some crazy ideas," Joe said. "Would you believe he wanted to fence off part of the bay as a refuge for stranded dolphins and whales?"

"You think that's something?" Frank replied. He tapped the page in his hand. "How about bringing in a pack of timber wolves as a way of controlling the deer population? Wouldn't the neighbors have loved that? Can't you just hear the howls of protest?"

Joe grinned. "Nope—no wolves, no howls." He dodged Frank's punch and went back to reading.

A couple of minutes later, Frank said, "Joe, listen to this. It's from the last letter Tanya got from Walter Parent."

I wonder if you possess all the cleverness and devotion to my vision that I expect and *require*. If you have both, I promise you all the resources you will need to succeed. If you fall short in either, however, I guarantee that you will fail. This failure will occur two years from today, my birthday. It is not the present I would have wanted, but so be it!,

Frank finished reading and turned back to the first page. "Joe!" he gasped. "This was written just under two years ago. Parent's birthday is a week from yesterday—that's next Monday—and now Tanya is worried that the center may fail. What if Walter Parent is somehow reaching from beyond the grave to *make* it fail!"

4 Tangled Relations

"Come off it, Frank," Joe scoffed. "Are you trying to tell me some ghost went downstairs last night and shoved around that stuffed elk?"

"Of course not. But ghosts can have help, you know," Frank retorted, stung by his brother's sarcasm. "What if Parent arranged for someone to keep an eye on the center to make sure it stayed in tune with his ideas after he died?"

"I get it," Joe said. "And if Tanya and her board strayed from the true path, Parent's watchdog— whoever he or she is—would be set to start a campaign of sabotage. That way, Parent's prediction about the center's failure would come true. It's possible, I guess, but it's pretty twisted."

"From everything we've heard and read, Parent himself was a bit twisted," Frank pointed out. "And what about his thing for puzzles? He loved solving them, and he loved stumping other people with them. Well, there's a real puzzle to set for everybody. How can a man who's started an organization go on controlling it after he's dead?"

"With something like a delayed-action fuse," Joe said. "Like that bomb they found in Europe a few weeks ago. It was from all the way back in World War II, but it was still dangerous."

Callie appeared on the front steps. She spotted Frank and Joe and waved. Frank waved back and motioned for her to join them.

"I've been looking for you guys," Callie said, settling down on the grass. "I tried to catch you after the seminar, but Bruce got to you first. Joe, everybody's talking about your run-in with Carl during the night."

"What are they saying?" Joe asked warily.

"Some of them are wondering what Carl was doing downstairs at that hour, and some are wondering what *you* were doing downstairs at that hour," Callie replied.

"Did you happen to speak to Sal?" Joe asked. "Funny thing—when I got up to get a glass of water, he was gone. I wouldn't mind knowing where he was."

"Sorry, can't help you," Callie said. "Why don't you ask him?"

"I will," Joe said. "But I need to figure out how to do it without sounding too much like a detective and blowing our cover."

"Do you think you'll get anywhere with this case?" Callie asked.

"We're already getting somewhere," Frank replied. "The problem is, we're not quite sure where." He told her about the hidden compartment in the exhibit room wall, the call from the television station, and the threat in Parent's last letter.

As she listened, Callie plucked a blade of grass and chewed on it. "Hmm," she said, when Frank finished. "So you think maybe Parent asked somebody to see if the center carried out his wishes and to take steps if the answer was no. If you're right, there's an obvious suspect."

Frank nodded. "I know. Bruce Rotan, Parent's right-hand man. In fact, if we're right about the reason for the harassment, and if it couldn't have been done by someone from outside the center, he looks like the *only* suspect. The interns are probably too young to have known Parent, and I don't see Tanya trying to wreck the center when she's put so much of herself into building it."

"I don't like it," Joe said, shaking his head. "It's *too* obvious. Besides, how could Parent have been so sure Bruce would go on working here?"

"Easy," Callie said. "What if Parent told Tanya that he wanted Bruce to stay on? Suppose he even made it a requirement? It was his house and land, after all."

"We can check that easily enough," Frank said. "We'll ask Tanya. Callie, do you get along okay with

Bruce? Could you look for a chance to chat with him? Find out how he feels about the center's program, ask him what Walter Parent was like to work for, stuff like that."

"I can handle that," Callie said. "What are you planning to do next?"

"Work at getting to know the other guys," Frank said. "One of them might have some link to Parent after all."

"Or the sabotage might not have anything to do with Parent," Joe pointed out. "We'd better not make up our minds too soon."

From inside the mansion came the faint sound of a bell.

"Lunchtime," Callie said, getting to her feet.

The Hardys followed her inside and downstairs to the dining room. The fixings for salads and sandwiches were arrayed on a table at one end of the room. A gray-haired woman in a white apron came from the kitchen with a basket of chips in each hand.

"Hi, Maureen," Callie said. "I want you to meet my friends Frank and Joe. I talked them into joining the intern program. Maureen is the one who keeps the rest of us sane and well fed."

"Go on with you," Maureen said. Her cheeks turned pink. She looked over the table. "And here I am listening to your nonsense and forgetting to set out the vegetable sticks and dip!"

"Maureen's great," Callie told Frank and Joe.

"Not only is she a good cook, she's always in an upbeat mood. It's hard to stay gloomy around her. And wait till you taste her peach cobbler!"

They filled plates and took them to the table. Sal sat by himself at one end. Joe took the chair next to him. Frank and Callie sat across from him.

"Hey," Joe said. "You missed the excitement last night."

"I heard about that," Sal replied. "I don't know what you're going to think about this place. First you have to stop someone from braining me with a shovel. Then somebody jumps you in the middle of the night and tries to strangle you."

"What happened?" Frank asked, laying a trap for Sal. "Were you so tired that you slept through all the hoo-ha?"

Sal didn't fall into it. "Not exactly," he said. He hesitated, then went on. "The fact is, sometimes I wake up at night and the only way I can get back to sleep is to go down the hall and take a shower. That's what I did last night. With the water running, I didn't hear a thing. And then, as soon as I was done, I plopped back into bed and was out like a light."

"It's funny I didn't hear the water running when I left the room to go downstairs," Joe said with a casual tone in his voice.

"Well, maybe I had already turned the water off." Sal glared at Joe.

"I'll have to try taking a shower the next time I

can't sleep," Callie said as if to break the tension. "It sounds a lot easier than coming all the way down here for a glass of milk."

After eating in silence for a full minute, Joe decided to try another tack.

"What brought you to Shorewood, Sal?" he asked. "How did you find out about it?"

"I've always been into nature," Sal replied. "I've had pets and my own patch of garden since I was little. So when my uncle told me about this internship program, it seemed like a natural."

"Your uncle?" Frank asked.

Sal tossed his head to get a stray lock of hair off his forehead. "Yeah, Uncle Pete. He's got a landscape business. He used to do a lot of work around this place for old Mr. Parent. That's how he came to clue me in to the program. You might say he knew about it before it even existed. When we got together at Thanksgiving and all, he'd talk about Parent's plans for the estate. Some of them were pretty wild, I can tell you."

Frank remembered the wolf packs and the refuge for whales and nodded. "Does your uncle still do work around here?"

"Not much," Sal replied. "I guess the people who took over after Mr. Parent died wanted to pick their own landscapers. Too bad. Uncle Pete does first-class work, and this was one of his biggest accounts."

"Losing it must have been a blow," Callie observed.

Sal shrugged. "A blow to his pride, sure. But he's not hurting for business, let me tell you. All these big new houses going up, they look like nothing without nice lawns and shrubs around them. And once you spend the bucks to put in lawns and shrubs, you don't trust their care to some kid down the block. You bring in a pro, like my uncle."

Callie finished her salad and stood up. "I'll see you guys later," she said. "I've got some errands to do."

"Yeah, same here," Sal said. He stacked his knife, fork, paper cup, and wadded-up napkin on his plate and carried them over to the trash.

"So, what do you think?" Joe asked Frank in an undertone.

"His uncle has a motive to resent the center," Frank replied. "And Parent could have asked him to keep an eye on what happened here and make sure that it stayed in line with his plans. Maybe Sal's uncle urged Sal to become an intern so he would have someone on the inside."

"I wonder if anybody heard the shower running in the middle of the night," Joe said.

"So far we know two people who didn't," Frank pointed out. "You and me. That doesn't prove anything, though. The bathroom is down the hall and around a corner from the bedrooms. Let's go find Tanya. I'd like to get her take on Sal's uncle Pete."

Tanya was in her office. Frank asked his question. A look of surprise crossed Tanya's face. "Sal is

Pete Talignani's nephew?" she said. "I had no idea. Not that it makes any difference."

"According to Sal, it cost his uncle a lot of business when the center took over the estate," Joe said. "Were there any hard feelings?"

"Oh, I don't think so," Tanya replied. "Talignani is very good at what he does, but he's more accustomed to lawns and gardens than to wild habitats. He recognized that as quickly as we did."

"So he wouldn't have any reason to want to undermine the work of the center?" Frank asked.

"I don't think so," Tanya said. "Though to be frank, I can't imagine why anyone would want to undermine our work. We do so much good, and we do not harm anyone."

"Yesterday you mentioned some protests from neighbors," Joe said.

Tanya dismissed the protesters with a wave of her hand. "One never has unanimous approval for anything," she said. "I have even had letters complaining that the presence of stuffed animal specimens in our dioramas is an insult to the dignity of nonhuman species. I send them a polite note thanking them for their suggestions and think no more about it."

"Do you still have these letters?" Frank asked. "One of the writers might be upset or unbalanced enough to do something. We should check this out."

"I'll hunt them up and put them aside for you," Tanya promised.

"Oh, another thing," Joe said. "Whose idea was it for Bruce to stay on as your assistant?"

"Mine," Tanya replied, sounding surprised. "It seemed an obvious move. Why?"

"Parent didn't will him to you?" Frank pursued. "Tell you to be sure to keep him on, or something like that?"

Tanya shook her head decisively. "Not at all. If anything, I believe he was becoming distinctly cool to Bruce toward the end. Not that that means anything. Walter had more than his share of whims."

In the hallway, a buzzer sounded.

"We're opening for the afternoon," Tanya said. "Is there anything else? I have some calls to make."

"No, that's it for now," Frank said. He and Joe left her office. As they started down the corridor toward the entrance hall, they heard a confused murmur that turned into shouts and screams.

"Come on," Joe said, breaking into a run.

Frank followed his brother in the direction of the exhibit rooms. As they crossed the entrance hall, half a dozen people came bursting out of the first exhibit room. They were coughing and holding their hands over their faces. One of them was Wendy.

"What is it?" Frank asked her urgently. "What happened?"

Gasping, Wendy did not answer. Weakly, she waved her hand in the direction of the doorway.

Frank and Joe forced their way through the small

41

crowd and dashed through the first exhibit room to the entrance to the second.

From the doorway, Frank looked around urgently. Was one of the trash baskets in flames? Had a pipe broken and caused a flood? Was there a poisonous snake under one of the display cases?

Nothing seemed wrong. Relieved, Frank took a deep breath. Immediately, he felt as if someone had punched him in the stomach. The room reeked with the gut-wrenching stench of skunk.

5 Tracking the Scent

"Yuck! Let's get out of here!" Joe pressed his cupped hands over his nose and mouth. It didn't help. The terrible smell seeped through his tightly closed fingers.

He and Frank ran back to the entrance hall. Wendy had thrown open the large front doors. The visitors she had been guiding, wide-eyed and pale, were outside on the lawn. Two little groups were already hurrying in the direction of the public parking lot.

"Our attendance figures are going to drop through the basement this afternoon," Frank muttered.

"Maybe that's the idea," Joe replied. The air flowing in the doors felt sweet and fresh. He took a deep breath. Mistake—a change in the breeze brought him a new wave of skunk smell from behind him.

"What on earth—" Bruce came rushing down the hall from the office wing. Tanya was close behind him.

Bruce dashed into the exhibit rooms and immediately ran out again. "Where's Carl?" he demanded, choking. "We're going to need his help."

"He's on his way," Tanya replied. "I gave him an urgent beep on the way out of my office."

As she spoke, Joe spotted the khaki-clad caretaker striding across the lawn toward the house. He hurried up the steps and took a sniff. "Had a little visitor, did we? How did the critter get inside?"

"We'll worry about that later," Bruce said. "Get the windows open in there and see about setting up some fans."

Carl nodded. Pulling a blue bandanna from his hip pocket, he folded it over his nose and went through the doorway. Joe caught Frank's eye and gestured with his head. Holding their hands over their noses, the two Hardys followed Carl inside.

The caretaker went to the first of the high french windows. He used a small key on his key ring to unlock it, then flung it open wide. Immediately the smell was less intense than it had been.

"Give me a hand here, will you?" he grunted to the Hardys.

Joe and Frank helped him force open a reluctant window. "When was the last time this was opened?" Frank asked.

"Couple of years ago, I guess," Carl replied. "They're always locked. It's a question of security. My bosses keep promising to put an alarm system in, too. Just as well they haven't got to it yet, though. If they had, we'd have been overrun with cops the minute I opened this window."

Joe bent to peer under the furniture. If a skunk had found its way into the room, it was probably still there, he figured. It must be terrified. Would it let loose with another burst of spray? If so, Joe did not intend to be in the line of fire!

The only skunk Joe found had been there a long time. It was stuffed and in a glass display case, frozen forever in the act of digging for insects in a fallen tree trunk.

"You fellows keep an eye on things, okay?" Carl said. "Don't let any strangers in. I'll be right back. I'm going to go scare up a fan."

"I'm glad he doesn't hold last night against me," Joe said to Frank after Carl had left.

Frank didn't seem to hear. He was standing next to the skunk display, staring at the floor.

"What is it?" Joe demanded. "What did you find?"

Frank got down on one knee. "Look," he said, pointing to the area of the floor just behind the display case. "I don't think we have to worry about chasing a live skunk from the room."

Joe bent down. The skunk odor got stronger. He held his breath and looked to the spot where Frank was pointing. There on the floor was a small uncapped bottle lying on its side. The label showed a cartoon drawing of a grinning, winking skunk. Black thread encircled the neck of the bottle.

"The prankster strikes again," Joe murmured. He scanned the area. Just across the doorway from the display case was an old-fashioned radiator. A length of black thread dangled from one of the legs. He pulled it loose and examined it closely. It wasn't ordinary cotton sewing thread. It looked like very fine black nylon fishing leader.

"So simple," Frank said, when Joe showed him the second piece of thread. "The thread's across the doorway, invisible against the floor. The first person who walks through breaks it and tips over the bottle of skunk scent. You see what that means?"

Joe nodded. "Uh-huh. We had people back and forth through these rooms all morning. So the booby trap must have been set during the lunch break. But the building was closed then. The only people around were us—the interns and staff. That makes this definitely an inside job."

"I wonder how hard it is to find skunk scent," Frank said. "There's no brand or maker's name on the label, but it looks like something you'd find in a novelty shop. We'd better check around to see what we can find out."

"Good idea," Joe said. "Maybe the bad guy slipped up and left a trail we can follow."

Carl reappeared, carrying a window fan in one hand and a bucket of powerful disinfectant cleanser in the other. He had a mop tucked under one arm.

"Here, will you take this?" Carl asked. Joe took the fan from him and set it beside one of the open windows, facing out. While he plugged it in, Frank showed Carl the overturned bottle.

"So it wasn't a real skunk after all," Carl said. "You ask me, whoever did this is a lot worse skunk than any you're likely to find in the woods."

He dipped the mop in the cleaning solution and went to work scrubbing the floor. "This disinfectant will clean off some of the spray and will mask some of the odor."

Joe and Frank returned to the entrance hall. It was empty. Everyone had been driven outside by the smell. They stepped outside, too. Callie hurried over.

"Whew!" she said, wrinkling her nose. "You guys were in there too long! Better go wash and change, before some visitor gets a whiff of you."

Tanya joined them. Joe noticed that she stayed a couple of feet away. "What terrible luck," she said. "We'll have to close the interior for the rest of the day."

"It wasn't exactly luck," Frank said. He told her about the bottle of scent.

Tanya's face grew hard. "I see," she said, in a voice that oozed cold anger.

"We'll do what we can to stop whoever's behind this," Joe quickly assured her.

"I know you will," she said, with a little shake. "Thank you. Please excuse me. My board members must know about this latest outrage."

She walked inside. A moment later Bruce came over. "You fellows," he began. Then he made a face. "You both need a shower. Then I want you to tag along and help out with tours. Frank, I've assigned you to Wendy's group. Joe, you'll be with Rahsaan."

Bruce sniffed a couple of times and continued, "I'll let them know that you'll be a little delayed. Our schedule's already out the window anyway. Oh—and when you change out of those clothes, seal them in plastic bags, if you don't mind."

The Hardys went inside. "Funny," Joe said as they started up the stairs. "I don't smell a thing!"

Half an hour before dinner, Frank, Joe, and Callie met outside the building.

"We need to make some plans," Frank said.

"Let's go up the Red Arrow Trail," Callie suggested. "We'll probably have it to ourselves this late in the day."

The trail, which led through a marshy section of woods, was wide enough for the three friends to walk side by side. Its surface, a layer of wood chips, felt soft and springy underfoot.

"How did the afternoon go?" Callie asked.

Frank answered first. "I didn't have much time for detecting," he said ruefully. "Wendy was guiding a bunch of ten-year-olds along one of the nature trails. What she had to say was interesting, but I couldn't really listen. I was too busy playing sheepdog, keeping the flock together. Those kids wander off the minute your back is turned!"

Callie laughed. "I know. I've had groups like that myself. I hope you didn't let any of them bother the animals."

"It was touch and go," Frank replied. "One boy wanted to throw pebbles at a woodchuck. He changed his mind when Dylan told him woodchucks attack people. Do they, by the way?"

"Certainly not," Callie said indignantly. "They're the most harmless creatures around! Like any animal, they'll defend themselves if they're attacked. But if they have a choice, they run away. Dylan had no business saying a thing like that."

"Who is he anyway?" Joe asked.

"A guy," Callie said with a shrug. "He showed up one day a couple of weeks ago to take the tour. He and Wendy hit it off, and he's been hanging around ever since. How was your afternoon, Joe?"

"It had its moments," Joe said. "We had this loudmouth in the group. Every time Rahsaan tried to explain something, he jumped in with his own version. Rahsaan kept his cool, though. I don't think I would have. The guy was a royal pain."

"You get all kinds," Callie observed. "Most people appreciate what we're doing. They come here to enjoy nature and to learn. I try to keep that in mind when I run into one of the other type. I think what Shorewood is trying to do is important. That's why I'm so furious at whoever's trying to wreck it."

"We're getting somewhere," Frank told her. He explained about the bottle of skunk scent. "So a visitor couldn't have set the booby trap. It had to be one of the people who was in the building during the lunch break. That means one of us."

"Or Dylan," Callie said. "I'm pretty sure I saw him during the break. But why would he rig up a stink bomb? For that matter, why would anyone?"

"We've already found one possible motive," Joe said. "You were there when Sal told us about his uncle. Maybe he resents the way his uncle was treated. And some of the others may have links to Parent or the center that we don't know about."

The path curved left and crossed a rustic bridge over a pond. As the three walked onto the bridge, they heard a series of *plops.* Ripples showed where frogs had jumped into the water from their perches on logs and lily pads.

Joe stopped and leaned against the log railing. Something about it felt odd. He looked more closely. "Hey," he said. "This isn't wood. It's concrete. It's just made to look like a log."

"Most of the bridges are like that," Callie said. "I guess Parent thought they fit in better."

"We should remember that," Frank said. "In a case like this, nothing may be quite what it seems."

The clock in the tower of the carriage house struck the hour. Joe counted to twelve and sat up. He listened to Sal's breathing. It was slow and steady. Stealthily, Joe pulled on black jeans and a black T-shirt and tiptoed from the room. In the hall he slipped his feet into rubber-soled sneakers.

A sound came from behind him. Joe spun around. Frank crept out of his room, holding a finger to his lips. He, too, was dressed all in black.

Silently the two brothers walked downstairs to the basement. At the kitchen door, they paused.

Joe put his head close to Frank's and whispered, "You're sure there's no alarm in this part of the house?"

"I cleared it with Tanya," Frank whispered back. "She gave me a key, so we won't have to leave the door unlocked."

Outside, Joe pulled a small but powerful flashlight from his hip pocket. Shading the beam with his fingers, he shone it on the path. He and Frank waited until they were a good distance from the building to speak again.

"You think Carl will come?" Joe asked.

"He did last night," Frank replied. "As that pain in your neck should remind you. The question is, did he arrive before or after you heard the noise downstairs? Maybe he really was trying to catch the prankster. But I'd rather know for sure. Here's the path to his place."

The moment they entered the woods, the night seemed to close in. Joe's flashlight illuminated a small oval of ground, but that made everything around much darker. Rustling noises came from the bushes on either side. Joe knew they were probably made by field mice, but they sounded loud enough to be lions and tigers and bears.

Joe ducked as he sensed, rather than saw, something swoop past his head. A moment later, he heard a faint *whoo!* from a tree behind him. He was sure the owl was laughing at him.

"Uh-oh," Joe said suddenly. "To the rear, march!"

"Huh?" Frank replied. "What is it?"

Joe tugged at his arm. "Up ahead on the path," he said. "Bushy-tailed and black with a white stripe down its back. I'm *pretty* sure its face was pointing in our direction, but should we take a chance? We didn't bring enough changes of clothes with us to tangle with a real skunk."

The Hardys retreated. If they patroled nearer the main building, they could still watch for Carl and keep an eye out for other intruders as well.

As they drew near the edge of the woods, Joe saw the paler blue of the sky through the gap in the trees. The reflection of distant lights turned the clouds a pinkish color. Near the horizon, beyond the clouds, a sliver of moon played peekaboo. The chorus of tree frogs swelled, then faded.

Joe and Frank followed the path onto the lawn. The three floors of the darkened main building loomed against the sky like a docked ocean liner.

"Should we—" Joe started to say.

The beam of a high-powered flashlight suddenly blinded him. A second light was aimed at Frank.

"Police!" a hoarse voice barked. "On the ground, facedown, both of you! Keep those hands in plain sight. *Move!*"

6 Targets of Suspicion

Frank stretched his arms out to either side, palms forward. The police officer sounded edgy. It was not a good idea to do anything that might make him more so. Frank knelt on one knee, then used his hands to lower himself to the ground. From the corner of his eye, he saw that Joe was doing the same.

"Stretch those arms out in front of you," the officer ordered. "Hold it just like that."

Frank felt two hands pat him down for weapons. His head was turned to the right. He saw lights come on in the upstairs windows of the center. People inside must have heard the commotion, he figured.

"They're clean, Mike," a new voice said.

"Okay, sit up nice and slow," Mike ordered them. "Who are you, and what's your business here?"

Frank took the lead. He knew he could count on Joe to catch his cues. "We're both interns at the center," he said. "I'm Frank Hardy, and that's my brother, Joe. We're outside tonight because we think the center should do an owl census. We want to make sure it's a practical idea before we bring it up."

The front door of the center banged open. Frank glanced over and saw a little knot of people hurrying across the lawn toward them.

"An owl census?" the officer named Mike repeated in a sarcastic tone. "You wouldn't be pulling my leg, would you?"

"What is all this?" Tanya demanded. She gave her name, then added, "I am the director of Shorewood Nature Center. What is the problem?"

Mike identified himself. "Somebody called us to report a pair of prowlers," he continued. "When we came to check it out, we caught these two guys coming out of the woods. They claim they belong here. They say they were out chasing owls."

Frank heard suppressed laughter from the group of interns clustered behind Tanya.

"That is quite correct," Tanya told the officer. "Joe and Frank are members of our intern program. They have every right to stroll through the grounds if they choose to."

"At this time of night?" the second officer demanded.

"If you want to study nocturnal creatures such as owls," Tanya replied, "you must do it at night. Is that all, officers?"

"Sorry, I'm afraid it isn't," Mike said. "Calling in a false report to the police is not a harmless prank. It can have serious consequences."

"I don't understand, Officer," Tanya said. "Who called in this false report?"

"Well . . . we don't exactly know," Mike admitted. He sounded unhappy. "The guy hung up without identifying himself. But we used Caller ID to check it out. It came from the main number of the Shorewood Nature Center. Our anonymous informant was calling from right here!"

The two police officers questioned the group, but no one admitted making the call or noticing anything suspicious. Frustrated, the police returned to their car and drove off.

Tanya raised her voice. "All right, friends. The excitement is finished. Let's return to our rooms. We have a big day tomorrow."

Everyone trudged across the damp lawn toward the house. Callie fell in alongside Frank and Joe. In a low voice, she asked, "Are you okay?"

"Grass-stained and humiliated," Frank joked. "Otherwise, just fine."

"What do you think, Callie?" Joe asked quietly. "Will the others buy Frank's story about us being out looking for owls?"

Callie hesitated. "I doubt it," she said at last. "Let's face it, guys. It's not the world's greatest *owl*-a-bi!"

"I'll get you for that," Frank promised. Laughing aloud, Callie dashed toward the door. Frank was close behind her.

Joe caught up to them in the entrance hall. The others had already gone upstairs. "Kidding aside," he said, "who sicced the cops on us?"

Frank's face sobered. "From what the officer named Mike said, we know it was a man."

"That lets out me, Wendy, and Tanya," Callie said.

"And you and Tanya were the only ones who knew our plans for tonight," Frank added. "Whoever it was must have spotted us leaving the building. Joe? Any ideas?"

Joe thought back. "I was sure Sal was asleep," he said. "I could have been wrong, I guess."

"And I was sure Jack and Rahsaan were asleep," Frank said. "But I could have been wrong, too."

"Hey, what if it really was a prank call?" Callie suggested. "Maybe the caller had no idea you were outside and just wanted to make trouble."

"'Fraid not," Joe said. "Remember? According to Mike, the caller said 'a *pair* of prowlers.' That's a little too exact to be an accident. No, it has to be one of our roommates."

"Or Carl, or Bruce," Callie said.

"Not too likely," Frank said. "Whoever called

must have noticed us sneaking out. But Carl lives just a five-minute walk on the other side of the woods. And Bruce's quarters are upstairs at the far end of the building. Unless they just happened to be on the spot, how would they have seen us?"

"My money's on Sal," Joe announced. "Too bad. I like him. But if it were either Rahsaan or Jack, he would have had to sneak out of the room to call the cops without waking the other one. I can imagine someone sleeping through one person sneaking out, but two?"

"Some people are naturally heavy sleepers," Callie pointed out. "We should find out how deeply Rahsaan and Jack sleep. Though they did both wake up and come down for the ruckus."

"And Sal," Joe said. "*If* he slept through my getting up, that leaves him out. I'll question him the minute I get upstairs . . . unless he's already asleep!"

Sal was waiting for Joe by the open door of their room. "Listen," he said. "I've got a bad feeling about what's going on. What are you and your brother up to?"

Joe spread his hands and shrugged. "We went out to look for owls. Somebody saw us and called the cops. By the way, was that somebody you?"

Sal's neck reddened. "No, I didn't see you, and no, I didn't call the cops. If I *had* seen you, I would have had words with you myself. I don't like the

58

idea of people prowling around in the middle of the night. There's been too much bad stuff happening around here lately."

"We asked Tanya ahead of time," Joe told him. "She said it was all right. Next time I'll be sure to clear my plans with you, too. Okay?"

"You don't have to take it that way," Sal said. "I'm worried, that's all. Come on, we'd better catch some zzz's."

Sal turned and walked into the room. As he went past Joe's bed, his foot banged into something that rolled across the floor. Joe went over and picked it up. It was a spool of black nylon thread.

"Where'd that come from?" Sal asked, over Joe's shoulder. "It's not mine. Hey, wait a sec. The guy who pulled that skunk stunt used black thread. Carl told me."

Joe was thinking the same thing. He turned and gave Sal a hard-eyed look. Then he realized Sal was giving him the same sort of look.

Joe tossed the spool on his dresser. "It's not mine, either," he said emphatically. "Somebody must have dropped it here."

Sal stared at him. His fists were clenched. He opened his mouth to speak. Then, shoulders hunched, he turned away.

As he tried to fall asleep, Joe found his thoughts going around and around. Was the thread Sal's? If not, who had left it in their room? The door was not locked. Anyone could have tossed it in. In that case, it was obviously meant as a frame. But who was it fingering—Sal or Joe? Maybe the person who planted it didn't care whom it pointed to, as long as it pointed away from him . . .

"Well, well. Look who's here," Rahsaan said loudly when Joe and Frank came down to breakfast the next morning. "Our two *night owls!*"

Sal and Jack laughed and gave the Hardys nasty looks. At least the two had found something to be in agreement about, Joe thought. That was progress.

Joe and Frank filled their plates, poured glasses of milk, then walked to the table. Wendy slid over to make room for them. "I think doing an owl count is a terrific idea," she said when they sat down.

Joe gave her a grateful smile. More than once, his being undercover had led to people treating him like an outcast. He was used to it. That didn't mean he liked it.

"So do I," Callie said from the doorway. She stopped at the buffet to fill a bowl with cereal and fresh fruit. Then she sat down across from Joe.

"Let's face it, guys, we're outnumbered," Jack said to Sal and Rahsaan. He tried to make it sound like a joke, but Joe heard the hostile edge in his voice.

"Did you enjoy the nature trail yesterday?" Wendy asked Frank. "I'm afraid the kids were a handful."

Frank laughed. "Some of them sure were! But yes, I enjoyed it a lot. And I learned so much. You have to be a real expert to lead a tour like that."

"Not really," Wendy told him. "By tomorrow you could be taking a group around yourself. The most important thing is knowing how to admit you don't know something. If you try to fake it, it shows."

After breakfast, everyone went to the seminar room for a talk about the tropical rain forest. Halfway through, Tanya came into the room and said, "Frank? Joe? Could I speak to you, please?"

As he and Frank got up to leave, Joe could not help feeling they were being sent to the principal's office for acting up. The others had that look he remembered from grade school—a mixture of curiosity, a little sympathy, and a lot of relief that they weren't the ones being singled out.

They followed Tanya to one of the smaller exhibit rooms. "This display case of birds' eggs," she said, stopping. "It has been moved."

Joe and Frank looked all around the case. They found faint marks on the dark oak floor, a couple of inches from each of the legs.

"You're right," Frank said. "It was moved."

Joe stooped down and tilted his head one way, then the other. "Frank, look!" he exclaimed. "If you catch the reflection of the light just right, you can see a thumbprint on the glass."

"You're right!" Frank said a moment later. "From the pattern of bumps, I'd say the person was wearing rubber gloves . . . not lab gloves, but kitchen gloves. This could be an important clue!"

Tanya shook her head. "We use rubber gloves for many tasks here," she said. "They are all over."

"Still, this may be an unusual pattern," Frank replied. "We should dust and photograph it."

While Frank went upstairs to get his camera and fingerprint powder, Joe examined the wall behind the display case. He looked closely at each molding. Even so, he nearly missed a hairline crack. He began pressing on the wood in different places. Just as Frank returned, a panel swung open.

"Did you find anything?" Frank demanded excitedly.

Joe straightened up and cleared his throat. "Yeah," he said. "A stack of *Life* magazines from the 1950s, and about four tons of dust!"

Before Frank could respond, a bell clanged loudly from nearby.

Tanya gasped. "That's the fire alarm!"

Joe and Frank ran toward the central hall. It was already filling with dense black smoke. Joe threw himself to his hands and knees and peered under the layer of smoke. Dimly he spotted a bundle of clothes piled in the middle of the hall. Was that what was on fire?

Suddenly Joe felt a chill down his back. That wasn't a bundle of clothes. It was Sal! He was lying curled up on the floor—not moving and not breathing.

7 Piercing the Smoke Screen

The thick greasy smoke billowed through the entrance hall. Frank dived to the floor. There was still a layer of breathable air there, but it was no more than nine inches deep.

"Joe—get Sal!" he shouted. "I'll try to find the source of the fire."

Tanya said, "I'll make sure the others have left the building."

Joe was already on his way. He pulled himself across the hall on his belly, using his hands and feet. Frank followed him. He took slow, shallow breaths and tried to see where the smoke was coming from.

By now Joe had reached Sal. In quick glimpses, Frank saw him hook a hand under the unconscious boy's armpit and crawl toward the front door. Frank felt a surge of relief. The most urgent part of the job was done.

Now for Frank's part. He steered toward the densest part of the smoke. His eyes stung. He blinked repeatedly, trying to lessen the pain. Through a mist of tears, he saw, near the far wall, a black metal object about the size of a gallon paint can. It looked as if the smoke was billowing from an opening in the top of the thing.

Frank crawled faster. When he was a few feet away, he saw a chain attached to the neck of the object. Dangling from it was a metal cap a little wider than the opening. Frank touched a fingertip quickly to the cap. It was hot, but not too hot to touch. Leaning on one elbow, he grabbed the cap and dropped it onto the opening in the top of the gizmo. Then, for luck, he banged it a couple of times with his closed fist.

The smoke stopped. Frank twisted around and started to creep toward the front door. The ache in his lungs got worse with every breath he took. He felt a cough rising from his chest and forced it back. If he started coughing, he was afraid he wouldn't be able to stop.

Frank could hear the blare of sirens and truck horns outside. Boots pounded up the front steps. Two sets of hands grasped Frank by the arms and tugged him out the door into the sunlight and fresh air.

"I'm all right," he started to say. The effort of

speaking set off the cough he had been holding back.

"Here. This'll help." A woman in a white jacket handed him a small tank of oxygen with a clear face mask attached. Frank put the mask over his nose and mouth and took a couple of whiffs. It helped a lot.

"Thanks," he said, removing the mask to speak. "The others are okay, aren't they?"

"They're fine." The woman pointed to her right. Frank could see Joe and Sal sitting on the steps. Sal looked very pale. The other interns were clustered around them. Callie saw Frank and hurried to his side.

"How do you feel?" she asked, taking his arm.

"Smoky," he replied, rubbing his forehead. Some greasy soot came off on his hand. "I must look pretty wild."

"Well, yes," Callie agreed with a smile. "But you're safe. That's the main thing."

Three firefighters came out and down the steps. The one in the middle was holding the black metal gizmo in his gloved hands.

Tanya rushed over to them. "What is that?" she asked. "I've seen something like it before."

"It's a smudge pot," the firefighter told her. "It's filled with oil and sends out thick smoke. Fruit growers use them to lay down a smoke screen when there's a danger of frost."

"I thought it looked familiar," Frank murmured

to Callie. "I saw those in Florida one time, when we visited an orange grove."

"You mean there is no fire?" Tanya demanded.

"No, ma'am, just a lot of smoke," the firefighter replied. "Once you clear it out, you should be fine."

"Uh-oh," Frank muttered. "More problems on the way." A van with a satellite dish on the roof was speeding up the drive toward the house. Just behind it was a bright red sports car with the top down. A young woman with short blond hair was at the wheel. Frank had seen her face before, on television.

The van and sports car stopped a few feet behind the fire truck. Two guys in striped overalls got out of the van and started unloading video equipment.

The blond woman got out of her car, looked around, and walked straight to Tanya.

"Hi there. Kate Mulhare, Channel Eight news," she said. "I caught the flash on the emergency band and came right over. More trouble, huh? Tell me, is there a jinx on this place?"

"Certainly not!" Tanya said stiffly. "I must ask—"

"A skunk inside the museum," Mulhare said. "Furniture moving around mysteriously. And wasn't there a report of prowlers early this morning? When you add to that the eccentric reputation of Walter Parent—"

"—You get nothing that makes a news story," Tanya said firmly.

One of the camera crew came over and fastened a tiny mike to the collar of Mulhare's blouse. He turned to Frank and said, "Would you mind moving? You're in the frame."

"I'm sorry, you'll have to leave," Tanya said to the cameraman. Her face reddened.

"A fire at an important institution like this is breaking news," Mulhare insisted. "Do you want half a million viewers to watch you try to kick us out?"

A firefighter with pairs of silver bars on the collar of his shirt walked up to Tanya. "We'll be on our way," he said. "I'd keep an eye out if I were you. Somebody around here has a nasty sense of humor. The chief will have to decide if we investigate further."

Mulhare gestured to her camera operator, then said, "A nasty sense of humor? What do you mean by that, Captain?"

The fire captain glanced at Tanya, then at the camera, before answering. "Somebody lit a smudge pot inside the building," he said. "Maybe it was meant as a prank, but it could have led to a very serious situation. The person who did it was literally playing with fire."

He nodded to Tanya and walked to the fire truck.

"Look, Ms. Mulhare," Tanya began. Frank heard a note of desperation in her voice.

67

"Please, call me Kate," the newscaster said with a sugary smile.

"Kate," Tanya said through clenched teeth. "We are very, very busy right now. It is already past opening time. If I agree to an interview—say, tomorrow morning—will you please go now and leave us to our duties?"

The sugar in the smile dissolved into triumph. "Why, sure, Tanya," Mulhare said. "Eleven o'clock okay? That'll give us plenty of time to put the story together before we air it."

The camera crew packed up their equipment. The van and the red sports car drove off. Tanya watched them go, then wordlessly went into the building.

Joe joined Frank and Callie. "What was all that?" he asked.

Frank filled him in. Then he said, "We have to find out where that smudge pot came from."

Joe gave him a smug look. "How about the storage shed near the old apple orchard?"

"Is that a wild guess?" Frank asked.

"Last week there were half a dozen of them in the shed," Joe replied. "Sal just told me. He and Rahsaan noticed them. They were looking for baling wire to repair a break in a fence. *And* Sal says they mentioned seeing the smudge pots that night at dinner."

"Hey, that's right!" Callie exclaimed. "I remember!"

Frank felt his spirits sink. He had hoped that discovering the source of the smudge pot would narrow the list of suspects. But it was no help. All the interns had heard about the smudge pots in the shed. And of course Carl, the caretaker, *must* have known about them. Who did that leave? Only Bruce and Tanya, Frank thought glumly, and they could easily have known about them, too.

Joe broke into Frank's thoughts. "I'll go look around the shed right now. If that is where the smudge pot came from, the culprit may have left some clues."

"I think we should try to find out where everybody was right before the smudge pot went off," Callie said. "If two or three people were together, none of them could have lit it, right? How about I ask around?"

"Good idea," Frank said. "And I'll try to track down that skunk scent. I hope Tanya doesn't mind my using her phone."

Callie shook her head. "You saw the state Tanya was in after dealing with that TV reporter. I doubt if she'd mind *anything* that might get her out of this mess."

Tanya put Frank at a table in her office with a telephone and two volumes of Yellow Pages. He started calling each of the companies listed under "Novelties." The first one offered to imprint his name and message on ballpoint pens. The second specialized in helium-filled party balloons. A woman at the third company didn't sell skunk scent, but for a very reasonable price she could have a picture of a skunk embroidered on baseball caps.

Frank dialed the next number on his list and explained what he was after.

"Skunks?" the man on the other end repeated. "How about stink bombs? Those I have. First class, too. They'll clear everybody out of a room in ten seconds flat."

"How do they work?" Frank asked.

"They're little balls of thin glass," the man explained. "You throw one on the floor and get away fast."

"Do they smell like skunk?" Frank pursued.

"They stink, that's all I know," the man said. "Really, really bad. I'm talking sickening. What is it with skunks, anyway? You're the second customer this week who wants skunks."

Frank sat up straighter. "Oh, that must have been my sister, Pamela, who called before," he said.

"Nope, it was a man," the dealer said, taking the bait. "I told him to leave his number and I'd see what I could do. No dice. He hung up on me."

Frank reached the end of the listings. No shop in either directory had skunk scent. One used to carry it but stopped because it didn't sell well.

"Around here, we smell skunk often enough just driving around," the shop's owner told him. "You might try New York City. People there probably think the smell of skunk is exotic."

Good advice, Frank thought. He went to the bookcase for the Manhattan Yellow Pages. While he was thumbing through it, the phone rang. Tanya answered. After a minute or two of conversation, she waved Frank over and switched to the speaker phone.

". . . your problems," a deep voice was saying. "I sympathize. But my offer won't last forever. It can't. From what I hear, the Shorewood Nature Center won't last forever, either. What you decide in the next few days will be critical to its survival."

"We have a splendid reputation," Tanya said proudly. "We're known throughout the East."

"Of course," the man said. "That's why I want to work with you. I want to help you, give you the resources you need to develop properly. My plan is best for Shorewood. I urge you, accept it now, while you still can. Otherwise, I take no responsibility for what happens. The center may be damaged beyond repair."

8 A Deadly Hang-Up

Tanya brought the call to an end. For a moment she leaned her head against her hand, with the palm shading her eyes. Then she sat up straight and took a deep breath.

Looking at Frank, she asked, "What impression do you have from what you just heard?"

"In one word? Menace," Frank replied.

"I see we agree," Tanya said. "That is some small comfort."

"Who was that?" Frank asked her.

Tanya picked up her pen and doodled on her desk pad. "A man named Douglas Cleland," she told him.

Frank thought he recognized the name. "The big developer?"

"Exactly," Tanya said with a nod. "The project he is most interested in at this moment is a new gated community of very expensive waterfront homes . . . to be built on the bay frontage of the Shorewood Nature Center."

Frank snapped his fingers. "You got a call about this the day we arrived. From somebody named Roger."

"That was Roger Mainwaring, the attorney for Shorewood," Tanya said. "Cleland approached him first. When we rejected his offer, he began calling me. The conversation you just heard is typical."

Puzzled, Frank said, "I don't get it. Why would the center sell its waterfront? And even if you wanted to, isn't there anything in Parent's will to stop you?"

"No. The trustees have the power to dispose of assets as they see fit," Tanya told him. "As for why, that is all too simple. Shorewood badly needs money. The land Cleland wants to buy is enormously valuable."

"Didn't you say that giving up that land would harm the center's program?" Frank asked.

"Yes, very much," Tanya said. She rotated her chair to face the window. "But if the board has to choose between selling the waterfront and closing the center . . ."

Frank was shocked. "Is the situation really *that* bad?"

Tanya turned back and met his eyes. "Doug Cleland is right," she said. "The choices we make in the next week or ten days will determine if

73

Shorewood survives. And if this harassment is not stopped at once, we may not even have a choice."

Frank's eyes widened. What Tanya was saying fit perfectly with the deadline Walter Parent had given in his letter. But what was the connection?

"Could Cleland somehow be behind this harassment?" Frank asked. "He may think the more trouble the center is in, the more likely you'll be forced to accept his offer."

"The idea occurred to me," Tanya said. She sounded tired. "So I asked a couple of people who've dealt with him. They both say he will gladly take advantage of our problems, but that he is much too concerned about his reputation to get involved in anything shady."

"Hmm." Frank was not convinced. He made a mental note to look into the Cleland angle. For now, however, he was nagged by a feeling that he had let some important fact slip by. What was it, though? Frowning, he played back the past few minutes in his mind.

"The center's lawyer," he began.

"Roger?" Tanya said. "Yes, what about him?"

"Did you say his name is Mainwaring?" Frank continued. "Any relation to Jack?"

"Why, yes, of course," Tanya replied, sounding surprised. "He is Jack's father."

"That's quite a coincidence," Frank observed.

"Not at all," Tanya said. "We just inaugurated the internship program this year. There hasn't been time for word about it to spread very far. So naturally most of our interns have some prior connection to Shorewood."

"The others, too, you mean?" Frank asked. "Wendy?"

"Her mother was one of Walter Parent's doctors," Tanya said.

"What about Rahsaan?" Frank continued.

Tanya nodded. "He was encouraged to apply by his biology teacher, who has been helping us design our school outreach program."

"And Joe and I uncovered Sal's connection. So the only person here who *doesn't* have a link to Parent or the center is Callie," Frank concluded.

"I suppose you're right," Tanya said. "I never thought of it quite that way. But what difference does it make?"

Frank shook his head. "It makes it a lot harder to figure out the prankster's motive. What if one of the interns is trying to wreck the center? The reason may go deep into the past . . . and not even his or her own past!"

Frank asked Tanya for a list of the trustees. Then he went down the list with her, asking questions about each of the names. He listened for something—anything—that might be a clue to a grudge against the center. Nothing struck him. Finally he went off to look for Joe and Callie.

They were in the dining room having coffee and freshly baked doughnuts. Frank snagged a doughnut off Joe's plate on his way to the coffee urn.

When he returned, Joe said, "So, a smudge pot is

missing from the storage shed. From the marks on the floor, all of them were shifted recently. I'd say someone used the others to top off the tank on the one that had the most oil."

"No lock on the shed?" Frank mumbled, through a mouthful of doughnut.

Joe shook his head. "There's a hasp, but no padlock. Just a piece of wood stuck through it to keep the door from swinging open. I asked Carl about it. He told me the area is off-limits to the public, and nothing in the shed is worth stealing. So it's easier to leave it unlocked. Moral? A five-year-old could have made off with that smudge pot."

Callie leaned forward. "Okay," she said. "But what about getting it here? You wouldn't want anyone to see you. And it's too big to tuck under your shirt."

Frank and Joe looked at each other. "Darkness," Joe said.

"Right," Frank said. "But you'd have to leave it somewhere between last night and this morning."

Frank finished his coffee and added, "How 'bout we go hunting for oil stains?"

As they started up the stairs, they met Bruce coming down. He gave them a steely look.

"Don't you three have anything to do?" he demanded. "I know we had a fire, but we can't allow that to throw off our whole schedule."

"Tanya asked us to work on a new project," Callie said. "We're gathering notes for a history of Shorewood. Can I talk to you sometime today? I need to ask a bunch of questions about Mr. Parent."

Bruce glanced at his watch. "I can spare you a quarter hour. Be in my office in five minutes."

"Thanks," Callie started to say, but Bruce was already disappearing through the dining-room door.

"Well!" Callie gave a short laugh. "I'd better grab that guy while I have the chance. You'll have to search for oil stains without me. Oh—don't forget to check the service stairs. There's a door to them at the back of the entrance hall."

"Near where the smudge pot was?" Joe asked.

A startled look crossed Callie's face. "I didn't think of that," she said. "*Very* near!"

"Let's try there first," Frank suggested.

They climbed together to the main floor. Callie pointed out the service door, then went to her appointment with Bruce.

Frank looked around. The smell of smoke still hung in the air. Carl had tried to wash the wall and ceiling, but it was easy to see where the smudge pot had been. The door to the service stairs was just a few feet away, set into the paneling.

How long would it take someone to pop out of the doorway, set down the smudge pot, light it, and vanish again into the wall? Frank wondered. Only a few seconds. Did that explain why the smudge pot had been placed in this particular spot?

Joe pushed open the door. They entered the

77

service area. Beyond the stairs, a narrow hall stretched off in either direction. The plain plaster walls needed a fresh coat of paint.

"If I were the bad guy," Joe mused, "I don't think I'd risk leaving the smudge pot in plain sight. Someone might notice it. Worse, they might decide it belonged somewhere else and take it away."

"Right," Frank said. "But the biggest danger would be letting someone see you *with* the gizmo. You'd want to leave it as close as possible to this spot."

A dozen feet down the corridor was a set of floor-to-ceiling cupboards built into the wall. Frank went to the first one and pulled open the door. It was lined with shelves. They held a variety of cleaning products with old-fashioned labels.

Joe, looking over Frank's shoulder, said, "That stuff would go for a lot of money at a flea market. It looks like it's been sitting there since 1900!"

Frank opened the next cupboard. It contained brooms, mops, and brushes. They, too, had an old look to them. The dust on the floor had been disturbed very recently, he noticed. He moved a wide push broom and looked behind it.

"Bingo!" Frank said. A dark circular stain about nine inches across had soaked into the wood floor. He bent down and touched it, then sniffed his fingertip. It smelled of fuel oil, the kind used in smudge pots.

He straightened up. "Okay. So the bad guy— let's call him or her X—brought the smudge pot here, maybe yesterday evening. This morning, after the seminar, X ducks in here, gets the smudge pot, and sets it off. Does that help us give X a name?"

"We weren't there to see who went where, but Callie was around," Joe reminded him. "According to her, Rahsaan stayed after to talk to the speaker. Jack and Sal went off on their own. So did Wendy. That means those three are still in the running."

"Rahsaan knows his way around the service halls," Frank said. "Could he have left the speaker long enough to run over here and set the smoke bomb going?"

"I hope not," Joe admitted. "It would be a real treat to cross *someone* off our list of suspects!"

They heard a door slam in the distance, followed by hurrying footsteps. Rahsaan came around a corner. When he saw the Hardys, he stopped short.

"*There* you are!" he exclaimed. "What are you doing in here? Never mind—I need your help."

"What's up?" asked Frank.

"Sal was supposed to lead a group with me in ten minutes," Rahsaan replied. "About thirty junior-high-school kids. But he's feeling sick from breathing all that smoke. Will you take over for him?"

"We haven't—" Joe started to say.

"Don't worry, I'll do all the talking," Rahsaan said. "I just need you to keep the kids from straying off and getting into trouble."

The Beech Grove Trail led through an area where the trees were far enough apart to let sunlight reach the forest floor. Rahsaan stopped to point out a patch of fiddlehead ferns.

"These are mature," he said. "But in the early spring, when they first come up, they're terrific in salads."

"Ugh!" a boy in a black T-shirt said. "Eat stuff that grows in the woods? Gross!"

"Yeah, right, Kevin," another boy said. "I'll bet you think your food comes from the supermarket."

"And milk comes from cartons, not cows," a girl with a brown ponytail added.

Kevin scowled. The rest of the kids laughed.

"That's okay," Rahsaan said. "For most of us, our food *does* come from the supermarket. That's why a place like Shorewood is so important—to help us get back in touch with nature. Come on, let's go see the duck pond. Joe, lead on."

"This way, everybody." Joe started up the trail. The group was close behind him. About thirty yards along, he noticed something odd ahead. A dead tree slanted across the trail. Its bottom rested on the ground, and its upper part was caught in the branches of another tree.

Joe remembered that lumberjacks called that a hang-up. It was one of the deadliest hazards of the woods. At any moment, with no warning, the branches supporting the dead tree might let it fall.

Joe stretched his arms to either side, blocking the trail. "Hold it, everybody," he said.

"What's the matter?" Frank asked, hurrying to Joe's side. "Oh—I see."

Kevin, the boy in the black T-shirt, darted past Joe's arm. "I'm going to get to those ducks first," he bragged, breaking into a trot.

"Hey, wait!" Joe shouted. "Come back!" He and Frank started after the boy.

Laughing, Kevin ran faster. As he neared the leaning tree trunk, he tripped and fell on his stomach. With horror, Joe saw the trunk start to fall. Kevin was lying stunned, directly in its path.

9 The Million-Dollar Log

Frank saw the danger instantly. He sprang forward like an Olympic runner pushing off from the starting block. As his powerful legs carried him along the leaf-strewn trail, his brain was doing a series of complex problems in rate, time, and distance. Could he reach Kevin before the tree completed its deadly arc?

Joe was matching him stride for stride. He started to bend forward at the waist and stretch his arms out in front of him. Frank suddenly realized what he meant to do. He was planning to grab Kevin by the legs and tow him out of danger. It might work . . . but the timing was so tight that even a moment's delay could bring disaster.

For a fraction of a second, Frank considered helping Joe by grabbing one of Kevin's legs. No—

the risk was too great. Instead of helping, he might make Joe's job harder. There were two ways to save Kevin. Joe wanted to move the boy away from the danger. Frank wanted to move the danger away from the boy.

The instant he made his decision, Frank put it into action. He visualized the tree trunk as an opposing ball carrier nearing the end zone. Tucking his chin against his chest, he dug in his toes and charged forward. His left shoulder struck the tree a solid blow. He kept his feet churning. In his mind he heard his coach yelling, "Through the runner! Tackle *through* the runner!"

Moments later Frank was sprawled on the ground next to the tree. The force of his attack had made it swivel on its lower end and fall along the trail instead of across it. His shoulder ached. He noticed half a dozen scratches on his arms and hands, but he didn't feel them . . . yet. He pushed himself up and looked around. Joe was a couple of yards away, helping an unhurt Kevin to his feet.

"I-I-I'm sorry," the shaken boy stammered. "I didn't mean . . . I don't know what happened."

"I think I do," Frank muttered under his breath. Aloud, he said, "Rahsaan, why don't you and the group go ahead? Joe and I will stay here and take care of clearing the trail."

Rahsaan gave Frank a troubled look, but he took

the suggestion. Soon he and the group of kids were on their way.

"Okay, let's get to work," Frank said. "Why don't you check the trail. I'll concentrate on those branches that were holding up the tree."

"You don't think it was an accident," Joe said.

Frank pointed at the fallen log. "Look—dirt and traces of decay all along one side," he said. "It was lying on the ground for quite a while. Once they're down, dead trees don't get up again unless somebody helps."

While Joe scanned the trail, Frank leaned back to look up at the place where the dead tree had been. It was easy to find. The bark of the tree that was still standing was deeply scratched just above a broken branch. The only section of the branch that looked strong enough to hold up a log was right next to the trunk.

"The log must have been propped up there," Frank said to himself. "Then, for some reason, it rolled outward. The branch bent, then broke. The log fell. That's all clear enough . . . but what made it start to roll, just as Kevin ran under it?"

"Hey, look what I found!" Joe exclaimed. He held up a length of black nylon leader. One end was tied to a wedge-shaped piece of wood. "It feels thicker than what turned up in my room, but no question, it's the same kind of stuff."

Together, Frank and Joe traced the path of the thin, strong cord. It had stretched across the trail, hidden by dead leaves. Marks on a stump showed where it had changed direction, up toward the branch Frank had been looking at.

"It was fiendishly simple," Joe said, shaking his head. "When Kevin tripped on the cord, it pulled out the wedge that was holding the dead tree in place."

"Yes and no," Frank replied. "The cord was placed a couple of yards this side of the tree. If whoever tripped it had been walking, the tree would have fallen well ahead of them. They would have had a good scare, that's all. But Kevin was running. That's what carried him into the danger zone."

"You're saying whoever set the trap didn't mean to hurt anyone?" Joe asked. "That's crazy!"

"I'm saying he wasn't *trying* to hurt someone," Frank retorted. "It's like the smudge pot. He wasn't trying to burn down the center, just disrupt it. But he was willing to risk a serious fire. Here, he was willing to risk having that log injure someone."

"Could one person set up this trap?" Joe wondered.

"That's the next thing we have to find out," Frank said. He went to the thick end of the log, locked his hands under it, and heaved. Frank was surprised by how easily he lifted the end. The other end, still on the ground, acted as a pivot. Once he had the end at shoulder height, he inched toward the middle, lifting as he went. Soon the thick end was nearly at the level of the broken branch.

"The closer the log gets to being straight up and down, the easier it is to lift," he told Joe.

"Now we know one person could have set this up," Joe replied. "Come on. Drop that tree somewhere clear of the trail and let's head back. It's time we got answers to some of our questions."

At lunch Rahsaan told the other interns how the Hardys had rescued a kid from a falling tree.

"That is so great!" Wendy said. There was a murmur of agreement from the others.

Jack frowned. "This was on Beech Grove?" he asked. "I was up that way yesterday afternoon. I didn't see any dead trees overhanging the trail."

"What time were you there?" Joe asked eagerly.

"Oh, four-thirty or five," Jack replied.

"Maybe you didn't notice," Sal suggested. Joe heard doubt and suspicion in his voice.

Apparently Jack did, too. His eyes narrowed. "Listen, you," he began.

"I've got a name," Sal told him. "And it's just as good as yours."

"Hold it, guys," Rahsaan said. "Take it easy."

Jack and Sal stared down at their plates. Joe thought they looked like little kids pouting after the teacher corrected them.

Callie, trying to smooth over the awkwardness, said, "We've been having more than our share of trouble. Sal, how do you feel now?"

"I'm okay," he mumbled without looking up.

"I don't understand what happened to you," Joe said.

Sal cleared his throat. "When I saw the smoke, I ran to see what was going on," he said hoarsely. "The next I knew, I was outside. I must have passed out. I guess I'm supersensitive to smoke."

"Where were you when you first saw the smoke?" Frank asked. "Were you alone at the time?"

Sal's face hardened. "I was in the hall. And yeah, I was by myself. So what?"

"Somebody put the smudge pot there and got it going," Frank pointed out. "I thought maybe you noticed someone hanging around."

Sal stuck out his chin. "Well, I didn't," he declared. His tone seemed to say, Make something of it!

Dylan was sitting next to Wendy. He looked at Frank and said, "You know, with all that's going on, the last thing we need around here is some guys playing detective."

Callie was taking a sip of water. She sputtered and almost choked. Then she turned bright red. Joe took a deep breath. Everyone had seen her reaction. Would they connect it with Dylan's comment and guess the truth?

"Well, *I* wish we did have a detective or two around here," Rahsaan said. He was looking straight at Joe, with an unreadable expression. "Maybe they could help us. It's no fun working in a place where everybody's suspicious of everyone else and going around sniping at one another."

Joe, Frank, and Callie finished their lunch in relative silence. Afterward they went back to the bench under the big oak tree.

Callie sank down onto the bench. "I don't get it!" she declared. "Why is someone trying to destroy Shorewood?"

Frank scuffed at the dirt with the toe of his sneaker. "In the motive department, two of the biggies are hatred and money."

"Or both at the same time," Joe added.

"That waterfront land is worth a fortune," Frank said. "Let's say Jack's dad is hooked up with this developer, Cleland. That could be a powerful motive for Jack to make sure Shorewood *has* to sell."

"Or take Sal," Joe said. "He says he's okay about the way his uncle was treated by the trustees. But what if he's been brooding about it and decided to take revenge?"

"Or Wendy," Frank said.

"Come off it," Callie scoffed. "What kind of motive could Wendy have?"

"Wendy's mother was Walter Parent's doctor," Frank replied. "She must have known him well. He could have given her the secret job of undermining the center if it strayed from his intentions. Wendy could be acting as her mother's agent."

"We keep forgetting about Parent," Callie said. "But I have a feeling he's at the heart of this mystery. Why did he make that weird threat about the center failing?"

"The one with a deadline that's coming up?" Frank replied. "Because he was afraid it wouldn't turn out the way he wanted."

Callie shook her head impatiently. "Okay, okay. But what *did* he want the center to be?"

Joe gave a short laugh. "Whatever he wanted, he sure didn't leave it the money to carry out his wishes. If he had, the issue of selling the bay frontage wouldn't even come up."

"Well, what did he do with his money?" Callie asked. "The center inherited everything, didn't it?"

"That's a really good question," Frank said. "We've been a little slow to take it seriously. I wonder if Tanya's in her office."

Tanya was in. Frank brought her up-to-date, then asked, "Do you have any idea what Parent did with the bulk of his fortune?"

"Dissipated it somehow," Tanya replied. She sounded bitter. "Starting three years before he died, he repeatedly took large sums of cash from his account. As much as forty or fifty thousand dollars a week. Occasionally even more."

Joe whistled. Then he asked, "Was he gambling heavily? Paying blackmail?"

"No sign of either," Tanya said wearily. "The only clue I have is that in his financial log, next to each cash withdrawal, he wrote the number forty-seven."

Joe and Frank borrowed the log and Parent's appointment books for his last three years of life. With Callie's help, they set out to trace any link between the dates of the withdrawals and the people he was seeing around those dates.

After half an hour, Callie said, "I think I've got something. 'AB.' It always shows up a day or two after a withdrawal."

Joe and Frank each dipped into a different appointment book. "You're right!" Frank said, with mounting excitement. "Who or what is 'AB,' though?"

They checked the A and B sections of Parent's address book. Nothing jumped out at them.

"We can come back to that," Frank said. "Let's see when AB first turns up. Maybe that will give us a clue to what it means."

They scoured the earliest appointment book, page by page. They had reached the middle of May when Joe said, "There, look! Written very small, 'AB,' followed by some numbers."

Frank put his face close to the book. "It reads 'seventeen W forty-seven.' Hey, wait . . . *forty-seven*, the same as in the log!"

"But what is it? A compass bearing? The number of a safe-deposit box? Was Parent taking all that cash and stashing it someplace?"

Frank shook his head. "Safe-deposit box numbers don't usually have letters," he mused. "And if that W means west, the numbers are much too small to be compass bearings. West is two hundred seventy degrees."

"Wait, I'm sure I've written numbers that way myself," Joe said. "What if it's an address! Number seventeen on West Forty-seventh Road, or Drive, or whatever."

"Try West Forty-seventh Street in New York City," Callie said, with a note of triumph in her voice. "You guys know what that is, don't you? It's one of the biggest concentrations of diamond dealers in the whole world!"

10 Acres of Diamonds

Joe skillfully steered the van through the morning commuter traffic. In the distance, the twin towers of the World Trade Center punctuated the hazy horizon.

"I'm glad we had a peaceful night," he remarked. "Maybe the prankster has had second thoughts and called off the harassment. That last booby trap did almost kill somebody."

"I hope you're right," Frank replied. He took a sip of coffee from his stainless-steel travel mug. His dad had given it to him. It was supposed to be insulated and spillproof. It wasn't. Luckily, the big green leaf emblem on his Shorewood T-shirt hid the traces of a minor spill. "There's another possibility, though. Maybe what he's up to now is so drastic that he needs extra time to set it up."

"The eternal optimist!" Joe joked. "Well, at least Tanya could call off today's visit from that TV reporter. There's nothing like having a news helicopter land in the bay to make the problems of Shorewood look less exciting." He braked to a stop and joined the long line of cars waiting to pay the tunnel toll.

Frank grabbed a cassette at random and stuck it in the van's music system. It turned out to be a tape of Japanese flute music Joe's girlfriend, Iola, had given them. The gentle sounds blocked out the rumble of engines and the blare of horns outside.

Soothed by the music, Frank let his thoughts wander. Where was this case going? He replayed the evening before in his mind. He was sitting with Joe and Callie. They had been studying a table that listed all the different incidents across the top and everyone at Shorewood along the side.

"We don't have everything we need to know," Joe had said, looking at the blanks in the table.

"That's not surprising," Frank had replied. "We can't grill people about their movements without breaking our cover. We know a lot, though."

Callie had studied the table, then scratched her head. "I don't get it," she'd said. "According to this, nobody has an alibi for all the incidents. But *everyone* seems to be in the clear for at least one of them."

"A conspiracy?" Joe had suggested. Only half-serious, he'd added, "Maybe Sal and Jack are really working together. The feud between them could be a put-on."

"Yeah, right," Callie had said. "Or maybe Wendy and Dylan are business partners, not romantic partners."

"That reminds me," Frank had said. "What's up with that guy? I mean, he's here practically all the time. What's the deal?"

"He's on summer vacation, and he wants to be around Wendy," Callie had said. "I think it's kind of sweet. I know Wendy cleared it. As long as he doesn't get in the way of Wendy's work as an intern, I guess it's okay with Tanya for him to hang around."

"Does he pay for his meals?" Joe had wondered. "Maybe Maureen's cooking is the real reason he stays. That chicken with mushrooms and sour cream last night was primo."

Callie had grabbed a pillow from the couch and threatened Joe with it. "Keep your mind on the subject," she'd said before tossing the pillow at him.

Joe's voice broke into Frank's thoughts. "About time," Joe growled. He pulled up to the tollbooth and handed money to the attendant. Minutes later the van was threading its way through the streets of Manhattan.

The Hardys knew better than to take a car into the center of midtown Manhattan. They parked in a lot near the Hudson River and caught a crosstown bus on Forty-second Street. The sidewalks in the Times Square area were jammed with people. Many of them stopped to stare up at the huge electronic billboards on the sides of the buildings.

A block farther east, Bryant Park offered a welcome glimpse of green in the middle of so much stone and concrete. Frank noticed hundreds of green metal folding chairs scattered throughout the park. They reminded him of the parks in Paris.

"If we're still stuck in town at lunchtime," Frank said, "we should bring sandwiches here."

"Great idea," Joe replied. He pressed the tape to signal the driver that they wanted to get off at the next stop, Fifth Avenue.

Frank and Joe walked uptown to Forty-seventh Street. The moment they turned the corner, they were in a fantasy world. Every shop window, on both sides of the street, glittered with trays of diamond rings, bracelets, and necklaces.

The address they were looking for turned out to be an office building. What looked like a single store on the ground floor turned out to be divided up among a dozen or more diamond merchants. None of them looked thrilled to see two teens come in.

The Hardys approached the first counter. A uniformed guard ambled over and stood nearby. Frank had a photo of Walter Parent in his pocket. When he reached for it, the guard casually rested his hand on the butt of his holstered automatic.

Frank explained what he wanted and showed the photo. The jeweler glanced at it and shook his head. "Sorry," he said. "I can't help you." He walked away.

One merchant after another brushed them off the same way. Frank and Joe became more and more discouraged. Were they following a false trail? They reached the last stall in the shop. An elderly man with a white beard and friendly wrinkles around his eyes was behind the counter. He listened to them and studied the photo of Parent.

"No one I know," he said with a shrug. "Mostly I sell engagement rings to young couples. Did you try any of the firms upstairs?"

"Upstairs?" Joe repeated. "You mean there's more?"

"Is there more!" the man said with a laugh. "This building has diamond merchants like rice has white! Upstairs is more wholesale. If your man was buying in quantity, that is where he would go."

Checking out the offices on the upper floors was a nightmare. The Hardys had to convince a guard at the elevators to let them go up at all. They started at the top floor and worked their way down. The jewelers protected themselves and their treasures with locked steel-plated doors and TV-equipped intercoms. Some simply turned Frank and Joe away. Others let them in but barely long enough to say they had nothing to say.

"We should have worn disguises," Joe grumbled, after another dealer refused to open his door to them. "Santa Claus masks, maybe. The reaction couldn't be any worse than we're getting now."

"Hang tough," Frank advised. He rang the bell at the next door. "Above all, look honest."

Joe must have succeeded. The door latch buzzed them in. Inside, the office was dominated by an old but very efficient looking safe. A man in his thirties got up from a brightly lit work table and came to the counter that divided the room.

"What can I do for you?" he asked.

Frank launched into his story. The man glanced at Parent's photo. Then he took a closer look.

"I know that face," he announced, interrupting Frank. "He used to buy from my partner."

"Is your partner in?" Joe asked eagerly. "Can we speak to him?"

"Arnold? He retired almost a year ago," the man replied. The Hardys' disappointment must have shown. He added, "Tell you what. I'll give him a call. Maybe he'll see you."

When he got off the phone, the jeweler handed Frank a slip of paper. "He says he can spare a few minutes. Here's the address. It's Arnold Borglund."

Borglund's apartment was a ten-minute walk away. Frank and Joe made it in less than seven minutes.

"Come in," Borglund said. With his foot, he nudged a tricycle out of the way. "My granddaughter is visiting," he explained.

Frank guessed that Borglund was in his sixties. He had closely cropped gray hair and blue eyes that twinkled behind rimless glasses. He led the Hardys into the living room, moved a box of brightly colored plastic blocks off the sofa, and said, "Have a seat. What's this all about?"

Frank explained.

"He's dead, is he?" he said when he saw the photo. "I thought he must be. I'm sorry to hear it. Olden was always pleasant to do business with."

"Who?" Joe asked.

"Walter Olden," Borglund replied. He tapped the photo. "Him. Oh, I see . . . that was not his real name, is that it?"

"You don't seem surprised," Frank observed.

Borglund shrugged. "In my trade, we have many customers who prefer to keep their private affairs private. Not many who buy on Olden's scale, though. He had excellent taste and *very* deep pockets. What is your interest in this, by the way?"

Frank told him about Parent's bequest to the Shorewood Nature Center and showed him a letter of authorization signed by Tanya.

"And now this nature center needs to convert the gems to cash, I suppose," Borglund said. "I would love to help, but I'm retired."

"It's not that," Joe said. "We don't know where the diamonds are. Until we spoke to you, we didn't even know for sure they existed."

Borglund's jaw dropped. "Is this a joke?" he demanded. "You do realize we're talking about a collection of hundreds of stones of the very highest quality. Why, for one of them alone I could pick up that phone right now and get a quarter of a million for it. And there are dozens more nearly as valuable."

Frank took a deep breath. "What would the diamonds Parent bought from you be worth today?"

Borglund stroked his chin. "I'd be astonished if it came to less than fifteen million dollars."

"Fifteen million dollars!" Tanya stared at Frank and Joe. "Impossible!"

The Hardys had rushed back from New York and were now telling Tanya about the amazing discovery they had made during their morning in the diamond district.

"Borglund seemed sure of his facts," Frank told her. "Parent spent a fortune putting together a collection of fine diamonds. The puzzle is, what did he do with his collection?"

"Puzzles!" Tanya said bitterly. "How that man loved puzzles . . . especially when he could use them to stump other people. And here he is, doing it to us, almost two years after his death!"

"Two years!" Joe exclaimed. He slapped his palm on his knee. "Parent said the center would have all the resources it needed if it followed his principles. But if not, it would fail in two years."

"And the two years are up on Monday, his birthday," Frank said grimly. "That's it, Joe! He must have meant that something will happen to the diamonds—unless we solve his last puzzle in time."

"Will you do it?" Tanya pleaded. *"Can* you? The work we are doing here is so vital!"

"We'll do our best," Joe assured her. He turned to Frank. "The person who's been searching the house—could he have been looking for the diamonds?"

"Could be," Frank replied. "If so, that moves Carl and Bruce to the head of the suspect list. They had more to do directly with Parent than any of the others."

"Why don't we give them a test?" Joe suggested. "We can go ask them about what Parent was like. While we're talking to them, we'll drop words like 'jewel' and 'diamond' into the conversation."

"And see how they react," Frank said. "Sure. It's worth a try."

He glanced out the window. Carl was trimming hedges on the far side of the reflecting pool. "We can start right away," Frank added.

It was almost dinnertime. Joe and Frank sat on the grass near the front door. They were waiting for Callie, who had spent the afternoon leading tours of the center's marshlands.

"I'd say the last couple of hours were a waste," Joe observed. "What did we find out? Walter Parent was an oddball. Duh! And neither Carl nor

Bruce blinked when you called Parent a diamond in the rough."

Frank smiled. "I nearly cracked up when you started talking about your friend Jules," he said.

"Was I too subtle?" Joe asked. "I figured, guilty knowledge is guilty knowledge."

"No, that was fine," Frank said. "I just—"

He broke off. Tanya was at the front door, beckoning to them. When they went up to her, she said, "A telephone call for you. Take it in my office."

Frank switched on the speakerphone. A muffled voice said, "Look under the seat of the summerhouse. Something you want is there." *Click.*

"Summerhouse?" Frank asked Tanya.

"An old wooden structure on Pater's Bluff," Tanya told him. "It has a fine view over the bay, but the bluff falls very sharply to the water. We're keeping the area closed to the public until we can install protective railings along the trail."

"We'd better check out this tip," Frank told Joe. "How do we get there, Tanya?"

Tanya traced the route to Pater's Bluff on a map of the grounds. "Be careful," she said as they left.

The Hardys easily followed Tanya's directions. They turned off Red Ribbon Trail onto an unmarked side path. The bay came into sight. The wakes of powerboats and water-skiers crisscrossed the blue water.

Joe understood why Tanya kept this path off-limits to visitors. It led right along the edge of the bluff. Leaning over, he could see the narrow beach and surf—damp rocks sixty feet below.

"There's the summerhouse," Frank said. The rustic building perched at the very tip of a protruding section of the bluff, with views on three sides. "You realize this is a trap."

"Sure," Joe replied. "Why don't we leave the path before we get there and come on it from the other direction? Maybe we can get a look at whoever's waiting to ambush us."

"Lead on," Frank said, with an ironic bow.

Joe edged past him. He had taken only a few steps when he felt the ground collapse under him. Caught off balance, he started to tumble down the steep bluff to the deadly rocks far below.

11 A Bush Too Weak

"Frank, look out!" Joe shouted as he fell through the hidden gap in the cliffside path. He twisted desperately, reaching out for something—*anything*—to cling to. The groping fingers of his right hand closed on the dead branch of a small tree. With a crack like a rifle shot, it broke off, sending him backward down the steep bluff.

One glimpse above him showed Joe that his warning shout had come too late. Frank, too, had stumbled through the gap in the path. He was a dozen feet higher than Joe, sliding headfirst down the sandy slope on his back.

Joe's shoulder slammed into an outcropping of rock. The impact slowed his fall for a moment. Instantly, the flexibility Joe had gained from years of practicing jump shots and karate kicks came to his aid. He flung his legs outward in a backward somersault and wrapped his arms around the rock.

The sharp edges of the rock dug into his bare forearms, but he pushed the pain aside. Using his powerful thigh and calf muscles, he forced the toes of his hiking boots deep into the side of the bluff. He reached out his left hand and grabbed a scrubby bush.

Just in time, Joe thought with relief. Frank was sliding past him. Joe stretched out and snagged Frank's forearm with his right hand. "Take my arm," he shouted. "Quick!"

Frank's fingers closed tightly just above Joe's wrist. Two seconds later, Joe was struggling to stop one hundred seventy pounds of plunging mass with one arm. It felt as if his shoulder were coming apart. Then Frank managed to find a toehold himself. The pressure eased.

Joe caught his breath and looked upward. He had climbed much more challenging rock faces in the past. But that was with proper climbing gear and a belaying line in case he slipped.

"Joe?" Frank called. "I'm letting go of your arm. I think I see a possible route up."

"I'll follow you," Joe replied, as he released his grip on his brother. Kidding, he added, "That way, if I need to, I can always catch you again."

"Thanks," Frank deadpanned. "My self-confidence needed a boost like that."

The scramble up the slope to the safety of the path took more than ten minutes. It left both Hardys panting and drenched with sweat. Frank stripped off his Shorewood Nature Center T-shirt and used it to wipe his forehead. It left a broad streak of dirt.

"I noticed something just now," Joe said. "A torn plastic trash bag."

"Litterbugs," Frank said. "They're the worst."

"Yeah?" Joe retorted. "Not as bad as somebody who'd dig a pit under a path next to a cliff."

"So that's it." Frank stared down into the gap in the path. "He dug a hole in the path. Then he stretched a trash bag across, held up by sticks, and sprinkled a thin layer of dirt on top to disguise it. Quick, simple . . . and almost deadly."

"You want to see deadly?" Joe said through clenched teeth. "Hang around till I get my hands on the turkey who did it."

Working together, Joe and Frank dragged logs and brush to block the path on both sides of the gap. Then they hiked back to the center. Callie saw them come in and hurried over.

"I was about to come hunt for you guys," she said. Her eyes widened as she saw their scratched skin and ripped clothing. "What happened to you two?"

Frank told her about the trap that had almost caught him and Joe.

"I know that path!" Callie exclaimed. "It's scary enough without any pits dug in it. We'd better let Tanya know about this right away."

The three went down the corridor to Tanya's office. Frank had the impression that a door farther along closed quickly as they came into view.

When the Hardys told Tanya what had happened, she was horrified. "This has gone far enough," she announced. "I cannot have you put yourselves in such danger. You must drop the investigation at once."

"That's doing exactly what the bad guy wants us to do," Joe protested.

"So be it," Tanya replied. "I can't bear to be responsible for anything that might happen to you."

"You won't be," Joe pointed out. "If something happens to us, the one who's responsible is the one who made it happen."

"Anyway," Frank added, "we hope to catch him before he can do anything more. You heard that phone call. Did anything about it strike you?"

"No, nothing in particular," she said, after a moment's thought.

Joe pointed to the Caller ID unit on Tanya's desk. "You didn't notice the number the call came from, did you?"

She shook her head. "I'm sorry. We installed that very recently. I'm not yet accustomed to checking it."

Her eyes widened. "You know, the person who came to install it said something about a record of incoming calls. Do you suppose . . . ?"

It took Tanya five minutes to locate the manual for the unit. It took her, plus Joe, Frank, and Callie, another ten minutes to figure out how to access the unit's memory function. Finally they pushed the correct sequence of keys and read off the number.

"But . . ." Tanya said. "I don't understand.

That isn't an outside number. It's a secondary line we have here at the center. It serves the garage and the maintenance building."

"You mean anyone can just walk into the garage and make a call?" Callie asked.

"Oh, no," Tanya replied. "Those areas are far too open. You have to use a code to call out from those phones. Oh—I see," she added, in a changed voice.

"Who knows the code?" Frank asked.

"I do," Tanya said. "At least, I have it written down somewhere. And Bruce. And of course Carl. That's the line he uses most often, since it serves his shop."

"It's too obvious," Callie murmured. "I think he's being framed."

"Maybe," Frank replied. He asked Tanya, "Does Carl know about this Caller ID unit? Would he realize that the number could be traced?"

Tanya shrugged. "I doubt it. He is—how shall I put it?—not very comfortable with electronic equipment."

Joe and Frank exchanged a glance filled with meaning.

"I think we'd better take a look around Carl's workshop," Frank said. "Do you know if he's still there?"

Tanya glanced at her desk clock. "He is supposed to be finished for the day. However, he mentioned to me that he had some work to finish in the nursery."

She rummaged through one of her desk drawers. "Here are the keys to the workshop," she said, handing them to Frank. "I hope you find that your suspicions are misplaced. Callie, would you mind staying a moment? I need to talk to you."

Joe and Frank left the building and walked across the staff parking lot. Carl's workshop was a rather plain one-story brick building on the far side of the garage and stable complex. A line of evergreens hid it from the main house. Frank found the right key and unlocked the door.

As he stepped inside, Joe smelled a blend of machine oil, wood shavings, and lemon. He looked around the big room. To his right was a long maple workbench. The tool rack on the wall behind it held an assortment of hammers, chisels, and screwdrivers, arranged neatly by size. A table saw, drill press, router, and wood lathe completed the woodworking area. The other side of the room was devoted to metalworking and was just as well equipped and well maintained.

"There's the phone," Frank said. He went over to an old office desk piled high with papers. "Joe, look at this."

Joe joined Frank and peered at the telephone. "Those smudges on the handset were made by a rubber glove," he said. "And look, you can sort of make out the pattern there. I'd bet they're the same as the impression we found on the display case the other day."

Frank had opened the top drawer of the desk. "So would I," he said. He pulled a pair of yellow rubber gloves from the drawer and showed Joe the fingertip of one.

"Someone may have planted them there," Joe pointed out. "Why would Carl try to keep his fingerprints off his own phone? It's only normal for them to be there. Besides, maybe he happened to be wearing rubber gloves when the phone rang and he just didn't take them off."

"It's possible," Frank said. "Though I might be more convinced if we were talking about gardeners' gloves. These are kitchen gloves."

"So what's your take?" Joe asked.

Frank rubbed his chin. "What if you're not an experienced criminal?" he said slowly. "You've read books and watched TV. You know when you do something wrong, you should be careful not to leave fingerprints. You're about to make a phone call that may send a couple of snoops off a cliff. So out come the rubber gloves."

Joe was troubled by Frank's argument. True, his first meeting with Carl had left him with a sore neck. Still, he couldn't help sort of like someone who would set up a workshop like this one and keep it up so well. He took another admiring glance around. Then he stiffened.

On the far wall was a rack of gardening tools. Every rake, hoe, and shovel was spotless. Like any really careful craftperson, Carl spent a lot of effort keeping his tools in good order. Recent sharpenings had given their working edges a faint gleam. The wooden handles were oiled and polished. There was one exception, Joe noticed.

"Frank," Joe said, walking over to the wall. "Look at this."

"This" was a short-handled spade with a blade that curved to a point. The edge was dull. Little clumps of sand clung to the blade. Joe took a few grains and rubbed them between his thumb and fingertip. They were still slightly damp.

"Used recently," Frank said. "Since this afternoon, when we talked to Carl about Walter Parent and mentioned diamonds."

"He could have gone over to Pater's Bluff right away and laid that trap," Joe said. "Then, as soon as he finished, he could have come back here and made the call to Tanya's office."

Behind them, someone kicked the door open. Joe and Frank spun around. Carl was standing in the doorway, carrying a stack of big reddish clay flowerpots. He stared as if he believed the Hardys were ghosts. Maybe he did, Joe thought. If their suspicions were right, Carl *had* just tried to kill them.

Carl's gaze shifted. He apparently noticed the yellow rubber gloves in Frank's hand. Panic flared in his eyes.

The powerful muscles in his shoulders bunched up. He lifted the stack of flowerpots high over his head. With a loud grunt of exertion and rage, he heaved the heavy clay pots at Joe and Frank.

12 Taking Care of the Caretaker

The stack of flowerpots hurtled across the room. Frank threw himself to the floor behind the desk. The heavy pots smashed into the wall and shattered. Fragments flew everywhere. One grazed Frank's forehead, just above his right eye. He put his hand to the spot. It came away with blood on it.

"Carl's getting away!" Joe shouted. He jumped up and sprinted toward the door. "Let's get him!"

Frank jumped up, too. He paused just long enough to grab some tissues from the box on Carl's desk. He pressed them to his forehead and ran out after Joe and the fleeing caretaker.

Carl had apparently meant to run to his car in the staff parking lot. Partway there he must have realized he wouldn't have enough time to get into the car, start it, and drive away. He changed course toward the main building. His lead on Joe was at least fifty yards, but he didn't have Joe's strength or speed. With every stride, Joe narrowed the gap.

"Carl!" Joe shouted. "Wait! We just want to talk to you!"

Carl sped up.

Frank's running wasn't up to its usual pace. Still, it was fast enough for him to keep Joe and Carl in sight. As he neared the front entrance of the center, he saw a little group of interns and staff outside the door, drawn by Joe's shouts.

Carl saw them, too. He angled to the left, away from this new danger. Joe changed direction to cut him off. When they reached the entrance of the formal gardens, they were less than five yards apart.

Frank pumped his legs faster. He wanted to be there in case Joe needed him.

Carl reached the edge of the reflecting pool. He seemed unable to decide which way to go around it. He stopped and whirled to face his pursuers. His right hand reached back to his hip pocket.

"Joe, look out!" Frank shouted. "He's got a knife!"

Still running full tilt, Joe feinted to the left, then dodged right and tackled Carl around the waist. The knife whirled upward and came down with a splash in the pool. The momentum of Joe's charge carried Carl backward over the stone coping into the pool. They made a much bigger splash.

Joe got back to his feet first. He had a solid grip on Carl's elbow. Frank stood on the edge of the pool and leaned over to take Carl's other arm. The caretaker made a half-hearted attempt at shaking loose. Frank tightened his grasp.

A hand grabbed Frank's shoulder. "What do you idiots think you're up to?" Jack demanded. "Take your hands off him!"

Tanya was among the group rushing down to the scene of conflict. "It's all right, Jack," she said. "Frank and Joe know what they're doing."

Callie pushed past Sal and Rahsaan. "Frank!" she cried. "You're hurt! You're bleeding!"

Frank had forgotten the cut on his forehead. He still had the wad of tissues in his hand. He pressed it to his head. It stung.

The others helped Joe and Carl clamber out of the pool. They were both soaked.

Carl looked around at the curious faces. Frank felt him start to tremble. He knew this must be an emotional reaction. The plunge into the pool couldn't have chilled Carl so much. Even with the sun almost down, the afternoon was still warm.

Tanya caught Frank's eye. In a low voice, she said, "Bring him to my office." She looked around at the little crowd. "All right. The emergency is over."

As if on cue, from inside the building came the sound of the dinner bell. Reluctantly, the spectators turned and went inside.

Bruce stayed where he was. "Do you need my

help?" he asked Tanya. "Whatever the problem is here, I know Carl pretty well."

"Thanks. We can handle it," Tanya replied. She started toward the house. Frank and Joe brought Carl along behind her. Bruce hesitated for a moment, then followed. When they went into Tanya's office, he continued down the hall to his own.

"Now. What is all this?" Tanya demanded.

Frank and Joe told her about the rubber gloves and the dirty shovel they had found in Carl's workshop. They also told her about his violent reaction when he found them there.

"Carl?" Tanya said. "What do you have to say to all this? Are Frank and Joe correct?"

The caretaker had recovered from his earlier state. Sullenly, he said, "If you mean, have I been looking around the place, yes, I have. Mostly at night. I like my privacy."

"What were you looking for?" asked Joe.

Carl pressed his lips together.

"We know you were searching for compartments hidden in the walls," Frank said. "The building is full of them. What did you expect to find inside?"

"Treasure, what else?" Carl said. "I know old Mr. Parent hid a treasure here somewhere. I figured I'd find it and turn it over to the center."

Joe couldn't quite hold back a skeptical snort.

"How do you know about this treasure?" Tanya asked. When Carl didn't answer, she continued. "If you are open with us, perhaps we can avoid filing charges against you. If not . . ."

"Okay, okay," Carl said. He looked frightened again. Frank wondered if Carl had had brushes with the police in the past. Or maybe he was scared because this was the first time he had strayed outside the law. "Mr. Parent liked to talk to me about it. He used to laugh about how angry you'd be when you couldn't find his money. And all the time it was right under your noses, if you only knew where to look."

"Did he tell you where to look?" Frank asked.

"I wish!" Carl said. "One time I said it'd be a shame if no one found the treasure. I thought maybe he'd give me a hint. But all he said was that he'd arranged for that. The nature center would have plenty of time to match wits with him. If they didn't solve the puzzle, they'd lose the money. It'd go to a fund for wildlife painters. Mr. Parent liked wildlife painting nearly as much as he liked wildlife. Maybe more."

"I see why you prowled around at night and disturbed the display cases," Tanya said. "But why force us to close the building with your smoke and awful smells? What was the point?"

"That wasn't me!" Carl protested. "Don't forget, I'm the guy who had to clean up after the dirty so-and-so who did it. And I can tell you, it wasn't fun!"

"What about the tree that almost hit a kid?" Frank asked. "You rigged that, didn't you?"

"I'd never do a rotten thing like that!" Carl declared. "You want my opinion? Take a good look at that kid Dylan. More than once, I've caught him where he shouldn't be. He was tapping on the walls and stamping on the floor. He probably set the stink bomb and smoke bomb, too. I don't know why."

"But you *did* dig the pit that almost sent us to our deaths," Joe said. "Didn't you? We found the shovel."

Carl looked away. "It was a spade," he muttered. "Most people don't know the difference. You were asking all those questions. I figured you were after the treasure. I wanted to scare you off. I didn't mean for you to get hurt, just scared."

Tanya picked up her phone and pressed a button. "Bruce? Will you come see me, please? Yes, right away. Thanks."

She turned to Carl. "Will you wait in the hall?"

Carl left as Bruce came in. Tanya gave a summary of the Hardys' discoveries and Carl's confession. "He'll have to go," she concluded. "After that booby trap on the cliff path, we can't possibly keep him on staff. If anything happened to a visitor or one of the staff, we'd be looking at a ruinous lawsuit against the center."

"I agree," Bruce said. "We should clear this with Roger, though. We don't want Carl suing for wrongful dismissal. As for this treasure business, we shouldn't take it too seriously. Whenever a rich eccentric dies, you hear tales of fabulous troves of diamonds hidden in the walls."

"If we *did* find a treasure, it would resolve our current crisis," Tanya said wistfully.

Bruce glanced at Frank and Joe, as if wondering

why they were in on this discussion. Then he said, "We need a real-life solution, not a fairy tale. We are lucky enough to have one available, if we act promptly and decisively."

"Cleland's proposal?" Tanya snorted. "In trying to save Shorewood, we would destroy it! After selling off the water frontage, perhaps we should clear-cut the forest as well. Then we would have given up both our *shore* and our *wood!*"

While Joe ran upstairs to change into dry clothes, Frank thought over Carl's statement. If it could be believed, his only motive had been to find the treasure. Why would he also try to wreck the center? If nothing else, the harassment attracted attention and made it harder for him to carry out his secret searches of the building.

If Carl hadn't set the skunk scent and the smudge pot and the deadfall, who had? Frank thought. And what about Carl's accusation against Dylan? No question, the guy was a riddle that called out for an answer. Was he hanging around simply because of Wendy? Or did he have some hidden purpose?

Joe returned, and he and Frank went down to the dining room. Dinner was almost finished, but Maureen made plates for them. As they headed to the table, Rahsaan approached Frank. In an undertone, he said, "If you dudes need a hand anytime, I'm your man."

Frank gave him a puzzled look.

"The nickel finally dropped," Rahsaan said with

a grin. "I remembered where I'd heard your names before. My oldest sister is married to a guy who's on the force in Bayport. You probably don't know him, but he sure knows about you two. Don't worry—I can keep my lips buttoned."

Frank and Joe took seats with Callie. By now the room was almost empty. Frank leaned closer and said, "Can you talk to Wendy? We need to find out what she knows about Dylan."

"I already thought of that," Callie replied. "We had a talk. Frankly, I don't understand her *or* Dylan. She's seeing so much of him, and she doesn't even know where he lives or who his parents are! He said he'd tell her everything in a few days."

"Tell me again how they met," Joe asked.

"He came to take a tour of the center," Callie said. "Wendy was the guide. They obviously clicked. The rest is history."

"So he could have come looking to worm his way into the center," Frank mused. "Who knows? If he hadn't found Wendy, he might have tried to hit on you instead."

Callie gave him an indignant look.

"Not that you would have fallen for it," Frank added hastily. "You would have known right away that it had to be an act."

"Exactly what are you saying?" Callie demanded. "That no one could possibly be attracted to me for real?"

Frank tried to think of a reply that would steer the conversation back into calmer waters.

Suddenly Frank raised his head and frowned. Was that a shout he had heard? A moment later any doubts vanished. Somewhere nearby two people were having a loud, angry argument. The words were muffled, but the emotion wasn't.

Frank gave Joe a quick glance and jumped to his feet. As he hurried toward the door, he heard a startled yell, a thunderous crash, and the sound of shattering glass.

13 A Crossed-Off Name

Joe, Frank, and Callie dashed up the stairs to the main floor. They found Jack, Sal, and Rahsaan clustered in the doorway to the first exhibit room, staring inside.

Joe edged through them into the room. Bruce was stretched out on the floor near the windows, looking dazed. Dylan was hunched on the other side of the room, looking just as dazed. Between them was an overturned display case. The dozens of geological specimens it usually held lay scattered amid the shards of broken glass.

"What has happened now?" Tanya wailed, pushing through the crowd into the room. "Is there no end to these disruptions?"

Bruce reached for the windowsill and pulled himself to his feet. Rubbing his cheek, he said, "I came upon this boy behaving suspiciously. I asked what he was doing here and reminded him that the center closes to the public at six."

He paused.

"Yes?" Tanya said. "Go on."

Bruce looked embarrassed. "Well . . . he threw a punch that caught me off guard. I stumbled against the display case and knocked it over, then fell down and bumped my head."

"You're a dirty liar!" Dylan shouted. "I never touched you!"

Wendy hurried over and took his arm. Dylan gave her a pleading look. "It's true!" he declared. "You believe me, don't you?"

"Of course, of course," Wendy replied. She sounded doubtful.

"Dylan? What just happened here, according to you?" Joe asked.

"I don't get it," Dylan replied. "I was hanging out in here, not doing anything wrong, just looking around. All of a sudden Bruce charged in and grabbed me. He started shouting that I was a thief. I tried to push him away. He deliberately turned over the display case. Then he flopped on the floor and pretended to be hurt."

"That's ridiculous," Bruce said. "What a feeble attempt to dodge blame. I don't know what you were doing in here, but you certainly acted guilty when I caught you at it."

"You didn't catch me at anything!" Dylan said. His voice cracked.

"That is quite enough," Tanya declared. "Young man, you are not a member of the Shorewood staff. You have no right to be on the grounds when the center is closed. I must ask you to leave at once."

"Wait, you don't—" Dylan began.

Tanya raised her voice and continued. "*If* you behave yourself, you can come back during our normal hours, when we are open to the public. If you cause any more trouble, I'll be forced to call the police. Is that clear?"

"But he's visiting me," Wendy protested. "Can't I have a guest?"

"Ordinarily, yes," Tanya said. "But he has abused that privilege. I'm sorry, Wendy, but I've made my decision."

Dylan took a deep breath. Joe thought he was going to try to argue further. But all he said was, "Huh!" He patted Wendy on the shoulder and walked to the door. Before leaving, he turned and said, "I didn't do anything wrong. I'll show you."

Tanya's shoulders sagged. "I don't know how much more of this I can take," she said. She looked down at the wreckage of the display case. "I must get Carl in here to put the room to rights."

"It's okay," Joe said. "We'll sweep up. Do you have a box we can put all the rocks in?"

Tanya sent Sal to find a carton. Wendy went over to her and said, "I know Dylan's telling the truth. I just know it!"

"I hope you are right, dear," Tanya replied. "But I cannot afford to take chances. Come with me. We'll have a cup of tea. Callie, will you join us?"

Jack looked at his watch and announced that he was going to watch a favorite program on TV. Rahsaan went with him. That left Joe and Frank alone with Bruce.

"Dylan's been hanging around for a while, hasn't he?" Frank remarked. "What was he up to tonight that made you suspicious?"

Bruce hesitated. Joe expected him to say that Dylan had been tapping on the walls. Instead, he said, "This may sound funny, but he was fiddling with that painting, trying to look behind it."

Joe looked where Bruce was pointing. The painting was hard to overlook. A weasel was crouched in the grass with its paw on a dead bird. It was snarling up at a red fox that was about to pounce from a rocky ledge. High above, a hawk circled, preparing to swoop down. All the colors seemed a little too bright and vivid to Joe.

"Did Walter Parent do that?" Frank asked.

"That's right," Bruce said. He sounded surprised. "How did you know?"

"It reminds me of that big painting of his in the entrance hall," Frank replied.

"Except this one's more true to life," Joe added. "No bears having a chat with turtles."

"Good point," Bruce said, with a short laugh.

Frank went over to the painting and tilted it up.

123

"Nothing here," he reported. "It's just a blank wall."

Sal returned with a cardboard box. He helped Joe pick up the geological specimens from the floor. Frank got a broom and dustpan and dealt with the broken glass. Bruce watched the cleanup for a few minutes. Then he went away.

When they finished, Sal went downstairs to join the others in the TV room. The Hardys had the exhibit room to themselves. They circled the room, testing every joint in the wood panels. Frank discovered one built-in cabinet. All it held were some old rags and an empty tin of furniture wax.

Joe gave an exasperated sigh. "Did Parent really stick millions in diamonds in the wall somewhere?" he wondered. "How crazy can you get!"

"*If* he did," Frank replied, "he must have left some clue as to where they are. Remember, Carl said Parent meant this to be a puzzle. Puzzles have solutions."

"He kept buying more diamonds until just a few weeks before his death," Joe pointed out. "Maybe there's a clue in his last appointment book. You know, like an entry that reads, 'Eleven-thirty— Hide diamonds in abandoned well.'"

"It's worth a try," Frank said.

Frank went to get the appointment book from the suitcase in his room. He and Joe sat at a table in the library and scoured it, page by page. After half an hour, Frank slammed it closed.

"Forget it," he said in disgust. "If there's any pattern there, it's too subtle for me!"

He dropped the book on the table. It fell open at the first page. Parent had neatly written in his name, address, phone and fax numbers, driver's license number, and blood type. The only blotch on the page was in the section headed In Case of Accident Please Notify. Something had been written in, then crossed out with angry pen strokes.

Frank held the book up to the light. "I can't read the name," he reported. "But there's a phone number. Take this down. . . ."

The computer in the library had access to the Internet. Joe and Frank logged on to a personal search site that included a reverse directory. Joe typed in the phone number and hit Enter. A few seconds later, the screen showed a listing for an Elaine Silver. The address was in a nearby town.

Joe stared up at Frank. "Silver? Isn't that Dylan's last name? Do you think . . . ?"

"Let's find out," Frank replied. He reached for the telephone and dialed the number. After a pause, he said, "Hi. Is Dylan there? Oh, okay, thanks. No, no message. I'll call another time."

The Hardys were silent for a few moments. Then Joe said, "Now we know why Dylan has been hanging around. He has some kind of close connection to Walter Parent. Remember, Tanya mentioned a distant cousin. What do you want to bet that cousin is Dylan's mom or dad? He probably blames the Shorewood Nature Center for doing him out of a fortune. So he's trying to get revenge."

"It makes sense," Frank said somberly. "Now the big question is, what is Dylan planning to pull next?"

"We'd better look for him," Joe suggested. As he and Frank left the library, they ran across Callie in the hall.

To Joe's question, Callie told them she had not seen Dylan since the scene in the exhibit room. "I know he's not with Wendy. I saw her just now in Tanya's office. She's pretty upset."

"Do you think she'd talk to us?" asked Frank.

Callie shook her head decisively. "Not a chance," she said. "She practically accused me of being part of a plot against Dylan, along with you guys, Bruce, Tanya, the King of Siam, and the U.S. Marine Corps Band."

"I get it," Joe said. "The old 'They're all against us' bit. Very romantic—like Romeo and Juliet."

Frank grabbed Joe and Callie by the arm and pulled them into an alcove behind a marble statue of a stag.

"Wha—" Callie started to say.

Frank put a finger to his lips, then pointed down the hall. Past the stag's neck, Joe saw Wendy. She had just come out of Tanya's office. She turned her head to look furtively up and down the corridor. Then she walked quickly toward the entrance hall and out through the front door.

"You want romantic?" Frank said softly. "How

about a meeting by moonlight with your banished boyfriend? Come on. Dylan may let her in on what he's planning. I want to hear."

The three friends hurried to the front door. Joe found the switch for the hall light. They didn't want it to betray them when they opened the door to go outside.

As his eyes adjusted to the darkness, Joe saw that there was still a hint of light in the western sky. The three-quarter moon was already high enough to light up the garden and the open area beyond. The encircling band of woods was black by contrast.

"She's headed for the reflecting pool," Frank murmured. "Is that someone waiting by the bench?"

"Yes," Callie whispered. "It's Dylan."

Joe and Callie followed Frank across the grass. They circled to the left, keeping the neatly trimmed shrubbery between them and their target. They stopped when they were close enough to hear.

"I told Tanya," Wendy was saying. Her voice quavered. "I swore you hadn't done anything wrong. But she wouldn't listen. She's like all the rest of them. They have it in for you because you're not part of the group. I can't believe they're so mean!"

"Listen, Wendy," Dylan said. "There's something I have to tell you."

"No, don't!" Wendy pleaded. "I can't bear it!"

"I haven't done anything wrong," Dylan continued. "But . . . well, I'm not really who I've been pretending to be. You see—"

He broke off and looked around. At that moment, Joe heard a noise like a giant blowing a lungful of air out through partly closed lips. A yellow-orange glow flickered on the bushes and trees.

Joe looked over his shoulder. The center showed in silhouette against the strengthening light. An alarm began to clang.

"Fire," Joe said. *"Fire!"*

14 Battling the Flames

Frank, Joe, and Callie jumped up and broke into a run. For a moment, Frank wondered if Dylan and Wendy would notice them. Then he dismissed the thought. This was an emergency. A minor concern like breaking his cover hardly mattered.

The flames shot higher against the night sky. Over the clamor of the alarm bell, Frank heard people yelling at the back of the mansion. As they rounded the corner of the building, he saw the source of the fire.

"It's Carl's workshop," he shouted to Joe.

Joe nodded and kept running.

Sal and Jack ran across the staff parking lot a few yards in front of the Hardys. Each of them was holding one side of a big metal reel of rolled-up firehose. Up ahead, Rahsaan was waiting, wrench in hand, next to a red fireplug.

Sal tripped and fell, letting go of the reel. Taken by surprise, Jack, too, dropped the reel, which rolled across the pavement in the wrong direction. Hardly breaking stride, Frank and Joe changed course and picked it up. They carried it to the hydrant and helped Rahsaan attach one end of the hose.

"Will it reach?" Joe wondered, eyeing the distance to the workshop.

"There's only one way to find out," Rahsaan replied. "Go! Yell when you're ready for water."

The Hardys started unrolling the heavy canvas hose. Jack and Sal ran up to help. Sal was carrying a wooden pole.

"Here!" he shouted. "We can use this as an axle!" He poked the pole through the hole in the center of the reel. Joe, on the other side, grabbed his end and tugged. Now the reel was a sort-of wheel. It rolled as fast as they could push it. The hose unwound as they went.

When the nozzle end of the hose came off the reel, they were close enough to feel the heat of the fire. The windows of the workshop were filled with flames. Part of the roof had burned away, allowing the fire to leap up into the branches of the nearest trees.

Frank took a quick survey. The line of evergreens stretched all the way to the garage, stable, and carriage house. Unless they stopped the fire now, it could spread until all of Shorewood was in danger.

Joe and Jack stood on either side of the hose, holding the nozzle with both hands and bracing their feet. Sal waved his arm over his head and yelled to Rahsaan, "Let 'er rip!"

For a moment, nothing happened. Frank had time enough to wonder if the fireplug was connected to a source of water. Then the hose swelled. Suddenly a stream of water as thick as a baseball bat shot out of the nozzle.

Joe and Jack staggered backward from the force. Frank wrapped his arm around Joe's waist to give him support. Together they arced the water upward, toward the smoldering branches. A cloud of white smoke appeared, and the licking flames went out. Nearby, somebody sent up a cheer.

The next important area was the roof. It took time to learn to direct the powerful stream accurately. Soon, however, they started to get the feel of it. As the flames seemed to retreat in one place, they twitched the nozzle and sent the water shooting toward another part of the blaze.

Frank focused all his attention on the fire and the water. Gradually he became aware that he heard sirens approaching. Three fire trucks roared into the parking area and skidded to a stop. Moments later somebody slapped Frank on the back.

"Okay, buddy," a voice shouted. "You've done your share. I'll take over now."

Frank gladly gave his place at the nozzle to the firefighter. His arms and shoulders ached from battling the force of the water, and his face and eyes stung from the heat of the flames. He stepped back and looked around.

Tanya was standing a few feet away. She had an arm around Carl's shoulders. The caretaker was staring with disbelief at the destruction of his workshop. Farther away, Wendy and Dylan were part of a bucket chain that kept the bushes and tree trunks damp. Others in the chain included Maureen, the cook, and several people Frank didn't recognize.

A man in khaki pants and a short-sleeved blue shirt came up to Tanya. "I understand you're in charge here," he said. "I'm Robert Crowell, the district fire marshal. Can you tell me if any flammable substances were kept in this building?"

Frank and Joe moved closer to the little group.

"I wouldn't think so," Tanya told the fire marshal. "This was Carl's workshop. Carl?"

"The main fuel tank is in a room off the garage," Carl said. "I kept a little can of gas in the workshop, though. Just enough to refill the weed trimmer and leaf blower."

"Was it closed tightly?" Crowell asked.

"You bet," Carl said. "That's not something I take chances with."

"Excuse me," Tanya said. "I have the feeling you are not satisfied about this fire."

"It's my job to investigate suspicious fires," Crowell said. "I don't think I ought to comment further at this point."

Frank turned to Joe and murmured, "The fire spread awfully quickly. When we first got here, did you smell anything?"

Joe nodded. "Uh-huh. Smoke . . . and just a trace of gasoline."

Before Frank could respond, Bruce rushed over to Tanya and Crowell. "Are you here investigating the fire?" he demanded. "I was one of the first on the scene. I was out taking a stroll and I spotted the flames."

"Yes, sir?" Crowell prompted.

"As I came up," Bruce continued, "I saw someone running into the woods. I recognized him. It was a young man who has been hanging around the center lately, causing trouble. Just a couple of hours ago, our director had to warn him to stay away."

Those within hearing turned to stare at Dylan. His mouth fell open. "I . . . I . . . that's a lie!" he cried. Jack stepped over and put his hand on Dylan's arm. Dylan pushed him away and ran off into the night. Jack hesitated, then took a few steps after him.

"Let him go," Tanya said. "We can find him later. Fighting the fire is more important. If he is guilty, the law will deal with him."

"He isn't guilty!" Wendy declared. "He was with me. He didn't do anything. And I think you're all horrible!"

Frank grabbed Joe and pulled him off out of earshot of the others.

Callie rushed over to join them. "Dylan didn't set the fire," she said indignantly. "We were watching him when it happened."

"We know," Frank replied. "Why is Bruce so sure it was Dylan?"

"Maybe he isn't," Callie suggested. "Maybe he simply wants to get Dylan in trouble. They had that fight before."

"In that case," Frank said, "who was it he really saw? Who torched Carl's workshop? Carl himself? He has a motive. Tanya fired him."

"Did you see his face while he was watching the building burn down?" Callie demanded. "He was devastated."

"People do things they feel sorry about later," Frank pointed out. "Maybe he's one of them."

"Hold on," Joe said slowly. "What if Bruce didn't see anyone?"

"What do you mean, Joe?" asked Callie.

"I haven't worked this out yet," Joe replied. "The center is in trouble because of all these incidents, right? So much trouble that it may have to sell the land along the water to that developer. Who's been pushing the hardest for Tanya to sell? Bruce. What if he's been pushing in more ways than one? What if the reason for the harassment isn't revenge at all, but to force the center to sell that land?"

Callie stared. "Are you saying that it's Bruce who

set off the smoke bomb and rigged the log deadfall and set fire to Carl's workshop?"

"I'm saying he has means and opportunity, and he may have motive," Joe responded. "I have to admit, I don't have any evidence, only suspicions."

"Wait!" Frank exclaimed. "I just thought of something. Remember when Bruce and Tanya were talking about what to do with Carl? Bruce made the point that when eccentric millionaires die, you always hear stories about fabulous troves of diamonds."

"Yeah," Joe said. "So?"

"Carl had just talked about a treasure," Frank said. "No one had even mentioned the word *diamonds!*"

Joe gave a low whistle. "So how did he know about the diamonds, unless he's playing some sort of double game?"

"I'm convinced," Callie announced. "But how do we find proof?"

"What if we track down the novelty shop where the skunk scent came from?" Joe suggested. "Maybe the people there could identify him."

"Or not," Callie said. "That kind of place must get lots of customers. Anyway, we don't even know if we'll manage to find the right one. What if he bought it somewhere out of the region?"

"Are you saying my idea smells?" Joe cracked.

"Smells . . ." Frank repeated. "I just had a wild idea. It's a long shot, but I think it's worth a try."

"What are you going to do?" Callie asked.

"Sniff the evidence," Frank replied with a grin.

Bruce was twenty feet away, still standing with Tanya and Crowell, the fire marshal. Frank walked toward them. When he got close, he stopped and knelt to retie his shoelace. His nose was just inches from Bruce's right hand. He took a deep breath.

The odor was faint but clear—gasoline!

Frank jumped to his feet. He reached out and seized Bruce's right wrist. Lifting it, he said to Crowell, "Smell this guy's hand."

Startled, the fire marshal stared at Frank. Then he took two or three sniffs. His eyes widened. Frowning at Bruce, he started to say, "Would you mind—"

Bruce tore his wrist out of Frank's grasp. Spinning on the ball of one foot, he brought the other knee up sharply. His target was Frank's belt line.

Frank twisted and took the blow on his hip. The force of it knocked him a couple of steps backward. He recovered almost instantly, but by then Bruce had darted away into the darkness. He was running in the direction of the parking lot.

15 The Puzzle Decoded

"What is Frank up to?" Callie wondered.

"I have no idea," Joe said. He watched Frank approach Bruce. When he saw Frank grab Bruce's hand, he understood. A grin took over his face.

An instant later Bruce attacked Frank. Joe's grin vanished. "He won't get away with that!" he growled.

Joe darted forward, then changed course when Bruce ran away. Jack was standing nearby, watching open-mouthed. Joe had to slow down and dodge around him. The maneuver cost him. Bruce was already in the parking lot, jerking open the door of a black sport-utility vehicle.

The starter whined. The engine caught with a roar. Joe told himself Bruce was just yards away from scoring a game-winning touchdown. Only Joe was in position to stop him. His legs pumped faster. Gravel sprayed from under his shoes.

Gravel sprayed from under the tires of the SUV, too. It lurched backward out of its parking slot, then accelerated toward the exit.

Joe pulled out a last burst of speed that allowed him to draw level with the SUV. He leaped onto the narrow step next to the rear door and grabbed the side rail of the roof rack. The side mirror gave him a glimpse of Bruce's face. His jaw was set and his lips were pressed together so tightly they almost disappeared.

Bruce's eyes moved to the mirror. They widened when he saw Joe hanging from the side of the car. Instantly he jerked the wheel to the right. Joe felt his feet slip from the step. The force of the swerve swung his body outward. It was like a nightmare ride in an amusement park. Frantically he tightened his grip on the roof rack. Bending at the waist, he forced his legs back and groped for his footing.

Bruce turned sharply back to the left. Joe slammed against the door. The door handle struck him just below the ribs, knocking the breath out of his lungs. For one moment he wondered how much more of this he could take. Should he jump off while he could still do so safely?

At the thought of giving up, Joe felt a savage growl rise from somewhere deep inside. He was not going to let this creep escape! Narrowing his eyes against the wind, he peered ahead. The single-lane road curved around the side of the main building. There it passed through a narrow gap in the hedges before joining the main drive.

Joe took a deep breath and started counting. One . . . two . . . On three he lunged forward, stretched his left arm in through Bruce's window, and grabbed the steering wheel. One well-timed jerk was enough. The SUV veered off the pavement onto the grass and crashed into the shrubbery.

Joe was ready for the impact. Even so, he lost his hold on the roof rack. He had just enough time to tuck his head between his shoulders and hide his face in the crook of his elbow. Then he smashed into the bushes. By the time he managed to scramble free of the tangled branches, the others had reached the scene. Frank and Rahsaan pulled a dazed Bruce from behind the wheel. The fire marshal used his car phone to call in the police.

Later, people gathered in the basement dining room. Maureen made cocoa and produced plates of freshly made peanut butter cookies.

Wendy paused in the doorway. "Tanya?" she said shyly. "Can I have a friend join us?"

Tanya smiled. "Of course, Wendy. Bring him in."

Dylan appeared. His jeans were torn and muddy, and his cheeks were scratched. Otherwise, he seemed okay. He glanced around the room and gave Frank and Joe a nod.

Once everyone had refreshments, Rahsaan said,

"Okay, let's have it. I don't understand anything that's happened."

"The ones to explain are Frank and Joe," Tanya said. "I should tell you that they are both very accomplished detectives. I asked them to come here, hoping they could help with our problems. They did everything I hoped for and much, much more."

"Detectives!" Jack said. "So that's it!"

"I knew there was something funny about you guys," Sal stated. "I have to admit, I had you down as part of the other team. Sorry about that."

Joe grinned. "That's okay, Sal. I had my doubts about you, too."

"But what about Bruce?" Wendy asked. "What was he doing? What was he after?"

"Joe and I took a look around his office a little while ago," Frank said. "One thing we turned up was a tape recorder connected to the phone in Tanya's office. Bruce was listening in on every call and every conversation. He knew why Joe and I were here from the first moment. That's why he planted a spool of fishing line in Joe's room, to cast suspicion on him."

"And that's how he knew about the diamonds!" Callie exclaimed.

"What diamonds?" Sal asked.

"We'll get to them," Frank said. "We also found a contract between Bruce and Douglas Cleland, the developer. If and when Cleland managed to buy the waterfront property from Shorewood, Bruce would get both a finder's fee and an interest in the development. That gave him a powerful motive to do whatever he could to force the sale."

"Bruce must have figured that if Shorewood got enough bad publicity, the trustees would have to sell," Joe said, taking up the story. "We're pretty sure he rigged the stink bomb and smudge pot and booby-trapped the trail. We found a receipt in his desk from a New York novelty shop. It doesn't say what it's for, but we'll call first thing in the morning. My bet is that it's for a little bottle of eau de skunk."

Frank said, "We think it was Bruce who made sure that local reporters found out about the incidents, too."

Tanya slapped her forehead. "Miss Channel Eight!" she said. "She is supposed to come tomorrow morning."

"Maybe the story of Bruce's arrest will take her mind off the center's problems," Joe said with a grin.

"Then it was Bruce who set the fire tonight?" Jack asked.

"Right," Frank said. "It was supposed to be one more example of the Shorewood jinx. *And* Bruce meant to use the fire to get Dylan out of the way."

"Why? What did he have against Dylan?" asked Sal.

"He must have noticed something familiar about Dylan's face and figured out who he really is," Joe said.

"Huh?" Rahsaan said. "Who is he?"

"Maybe Dylan should tell us that himself," Frank replied.

Dylan's face turned bright red. He grabbed Wendy's hand and held it tight. "Um . . ." he said. "The thing is, Walter Parent was my mom's cousin. We're his only relatives."

Tanya's eyes widened. "The distant relation," she said. "The family feud."

"Uh-huh, that's us," Dylan said. "I never knew what it was about. Face it, Uncle Walter was a little strange. Anyway, I came here because I wanted to hunt for a later will. I thought it might give us part of the estate. And now that I think about it, Bruce did give me a few funny looks."

"So Carl was right," Joe said. "You *were* poking around the house. Just as he was. You were searching for a will, and he was searching for a treasure."

"Well, I was looking for treasure, too," Dylan admitted. "When I was little, before he and Mom had their big fight, Uncle Walter used to show me the secret compartments in the walls. There was one where he kept a little velvet bag of jewels. If I managed to find the compartment and open it, I got to play with the jewels."

"Where was this compartment?" Tanya asked eagerly.

Dylan shook his head. "I don't know. I was really little then. I thought if I spent enough time around the house, maybe I'd remember. But it didn't work."

"This fits with what we discovered," Frank said. He told them about the missing millions in diamonds. "According to Carl, Walter Parent hid his treasure in the house and left the key to finding it in plain sight."

"It figures," Dylan said. "Uncle Walter was a nut about puzzles."

"He was a nut, period," Sal muttered.

Dylan pretended not to hear. "Every time I came over, he'd give me some new puzzle to solve. I remember, he was wild about rebuses."

"What's that?" Callie asked. "A kind of monkey?"

Frank laughed. "No, it's a puzzle where drawings of things stand for words," he explained. "Say you wanted to write 'I love you, dear.' You'd draw an eye, a heart, a capital U—"

"And Bambi," Callie said, breaking in. "Got it. I remember doing those in third grade. I can't imagine a grown man spending his time on them, though."

"He loved puzzles," Joe repeated. "And besides, he was a painter. Connecting words and sounds to pictures probably came naturally to him."

Frank stared at Joe. He could feel the pieces of the puzzle falling into place in his mind, but the picture they made was still hazy. Picture—that was it!

"Tanya?" he said. "That painting in the entrance hall. The huge one. Are Parent's other paintings pretty much like it?"

"Why . . . no," Tanya replied. "Not at all. In fact, I'd call it unique. We have a number of his canvases. They are all fairly realistic scenes from nature. The fox and ferret in the first exhibit room is one of the better examples."

"Then why would Parent insist on hanging such a weird picture in the most prominent spot in the house?" Frank continued. "One that shows an assortment of animals that would never be found together in nature?"

"Because he was weird," Sal suggested.

"Frank!" Callie gasped. "It must be a rebus!"

"The key that's in plain sight," Joe added.

Rahsaan jumped up. "What are we waiting for?" he said. "Let's have a treasure hunt!"

Everyone trooped upstairs to the entrance hall and looked at the painting. Frank could almost feel the discouragement in the air.

"I give up," Wendy said, after a minute or two. "A bunch of turtles, a bear, a bison, a sea lion . . . It makes no sense at all."

None of the others argued. Frank scowled. His idea had seemed so plausible. If it was correct, Walter Parent was a better puzzle maker than they were puzzle solvers.

"Look at those turtles," Tanya said slowly. "They are the most important elements in the painting. Why so many of them? And why are the markings on their shells so carefully painted?"

"I give up. Why?" Sal said.

"Of course!" Tanya shouted. "I am a fool! They

are not turtles. They are terrapins—*diamondback* terrapins!"

"Four diamondbacks," Joe said. *"Four diamond back . . .* Not four, *for!* That's it, Tanya! Now for the rest . . ."

Encouraged by Tanya's discovery, the others threw themselves into the game. Frank grabbed a notepad and pen. He tried to keep track of all the suggestions. Then he sorted them into three groups—possible, unlikely, and just plain strange. Soon every creature and object in the painting had been looked at, named, and made the object of bad puns.

"Okay, what have we got?" Jack asked.

Frank studied the page. "Say we read the painting from left to right and top to bottom," he said. "We get, 'For diamond back, bear right under stag.'"

"Hey, it actually makes sense," Joe said.

"So far, yes," Frank said. "But then we have 'Bison sea lion.' Not very helpful."

"Maybe we're being too exact," Callie suggested. "Most people call bisons buffalo."

"Sure," Wendy said. "And they call sea lions seals, too."

"Great," Sal grumbled. "So instead of bison sea lion, we get buffalo seal. Whoopdedoo."

"Tanya?" Frank said. "Where in the building is there a stag?"

Tanya thought for a moment. "We have a marble statue, life-size, in the east-wing corridor, and a

mounted head over the doorway to the third exhibit room. That room was formerly Parent's private
den."

"Let's go!" Joe cried, leading the way. The stag's
head was very prominent. Joe walked under it and
turned right, then stopped. "Now what?"

"Buffalo seal," Sal repeated.

Joe looked around the room. Like the other
rooms on the main floor, its walls were paneled in
antique wood. This room was especially elaborate.
The panels had medieval shields and coats of arms
carved into them. Most of the carvings were above
eye level. One, just to the right of the doorway, was
barely waist-high.

"A *low seal!*" Joe muttered to himself. He raised
his voice. "That's it! Buff a low seal!"

Holding his breath, he reached out and rubbed
the carving. As his fingers passed over the armor
helmet that topped the shield, he felt it move
inward. There was a faint click. A section of the
panel just below the shield swung open.

The shallow compartment behind the panel held
only a shoebox and an envelope. Joe took them out
and handed them to Tanya. She lifted the lid of the
shoebox. It was as if someone had just turned on a
floodlight. The box was half full of loose diamonds
that sparkled in the light. Most were clear, but Joe
noticed some with a blue, yellow, or pink tint.

At one end of the box was a stack of little brown
envelopes, held together by a rubber band. Tanya

took one from the stack and shook its contents into her palm. She held up a gem the size of a marble.

Everyone gasped. Tanya put the diamond back in its little envelope and closed the shoebox. She handed the box back to Joe. "Please hold this for me," she said.

Joe gripped it tightly. How often did he get a chance to hold fifteen million dollars?

"Well, now we know where Walter Parent's fortune went," Frank said.

Tanya had opened the envelope and was reading through the document it contained. She glanced at Dylan.

"We also know where his fortune is to go," she said. "This is a codicil to his will. It was not drafted by his usual law firm, and it was added after the original will was drawn up. He must have gone to someone else, someone who didn't know him, so that the document would remain secret."

"What does it say?" Dylan asked anxiously.

Tanya cleared her throat. "First, it cancels a sealed document he left with his lawyers that would have given the diamonds to a fund to further wildlife painting. And second, it bequeaths a portion of the gems to his cousin, Elaine Silver, and her son, Dylan."

Dylan let out a triumphant yell. He picked up Wendy by the waist and swung her around. When he finally put her down, he turned to Tanya. "Thank you! Is there any chance I could join the

147

internship program?" he asked. "I like it here, and I sort of feel I owe something to Uncle Walter."

"Well . . ." Tanya said gravely. "It happens that we have two vacancies coming up. Unless, of course, Frank and Joe want to stay on for the rest of the summer."

"No, that's okay," Frank said hastily. "It's been very interesting, but . . ."

"There are other cases people have asked us to look into," Joe said. "But we'd like to come back to visit."

"Any time at all," Tanya declared. "You will both be lifetime members of Shorewood Nature Center. And when the trustees meet, I plan to ask them to give you a token of our appreciation. The painting in the entrance hall must stay there, by the terms of Parent's will. But we have many others. If the trustees agree, you may take your choice."

Joe looked at Frank. He could imagine what their mom and dad would say when they walked in with a gigantic painting of a badger or an aardvark.

"Um, thanks a lot," Joe said. "We don't really need it, though. Being detectives is already enough of a *wild life!*"

THE HARDY BOYS® SERIES By Franklin W. Dixon

NANCY DREW® MYSTERY STORIES By Carolyn Keene

A MINSTREL® BOOK

Published by Pocket Books